MW01009431

CRUSH

CRUSH

a novel

ADA CALHOUN

:

VIKING

VIKING

An imprint of Penguin Random House LLC
1745 Broadway, New York, NY 10019
penguinrandomhouse.com

Designed by *Christina Nguyen*

Library of Congress Cataloging-in-Publication Data

Names: Calhoun, Ada, author.
Title: Crush : a novel / Ada Calhoun.
Description: New York : Viking, 2025.
Identifiers: LCCN 2024038405 (print) | LCCN 2024038406 (ebook) |
ISBN 9780593832028 (hardcover) | ISBN 9780593832035 (ebook)
Subjects: LCGFT: Novels.
Classification: LCC PS3603.A43865 C78 2025 (print) |
LCC PS3603.A43865 (ebook) | DDC 813/.6—dc23/eng/20240911
LC record available at https://lccn.loc.gov/2024038405
LC ebook record available at https://lccn.loc.gov/2024038406

Printed in the United States of America
1st Printing

The authorized representative in the EU for product safety and compliance is
Penguin Random House Ireland, Morrison Chambers, 32 Nassau Street,
Dublin D02 YH68, Ireland, https://eu-contact.penguin.ie.

For the love of my life

Every man has had one or two moments of
extraordinary experience, has met his soul, has
thought of something which he never afterwards forgot,
and which revised all his speech and moulded
all his forms of thought.

—Ralph Waldo Emerson

At the edge of the abyss he clings to pencils.

—Elias Canetti

CRUSH

ONE

To Crave and to Have

W e don't have to do anything," he said.

The first time I played Seven Minutes in Heaven at a party, I was locked in a closet with a boy I had a crush on. Romance in that era often involved vaguely sociopathic party games.

By the light of a blue bulb, I could see my classmate's wide-open eyes.

"I haven't kissed anybody before," he mumbled, with the shame usually reserved for having killed someone.

"Me either," I said, though I'd conducted a frame-by-frame analysis of the garage scene in *Some Kind of Wonderful*.

I reached out and found his face. His hand settled on my waist.

He was breathing quietly, like he feared waking a light sleeper. And then my mouth was on his. Soon we were pulling each other close, pushing hanging coats aside and sending empty hangers skidding across the dowel. We didn't know what to do, but our bodies did.

Then the door whooshed open. We squinted into the rec-room lights, Whitney Houston on the boom box. Our classmates, awaiting their turns, poured soda from two-liter bottles and trailed chips through ranch dip.

Thanks to that poorly chaperoned middle-school party, I discovered a whole new category of person, separate from friends and family: boys who would kiss me in closets.

I liked making out with them too much though. Later that year I was called a slut for kissing, in the span of three months, three boys—who, granted, formed a significant percentage of the class given the size of our school.

The social retribution for having succumbed to lust taught me one of the highest-stakes lessons of womanhood: Desire must be negotiated like furniture that's too big for the room. As I gradually rebuilt my reputation as a good girl—someone who was craved without craving—the lab report headline became, *How can I get what I want without actually having it?*

In high school I acquired an affable, stable boyfriend with whom I could enjoy state-sanctioned adolescent monogamy. I knew I wanted more, and I also knew that bad things happened to women who tried to find it.

In my Women's Literature elective, I underlined a passage in Marilynne Robinson's *Housekeeping*. It described just the sort of elegant self-denial to which I aspired: "To crave and to have are as like as a thing and its shadow. For when does a berry break upon the tongue as sweetly as when one longs to taste it . . ."

Wanting could be as good as having—even *better*? If true, that would solve a lot of problems.

By college, I'd found a way to have without holding, and that was flirting. This created energy without causing trouble, like a rolling boil in a lidded pot. I had a few crushes going all the time. There'd be one or two on the back burner simmering, a few in the freezer that could be stuck in the oven at 350 and ready to go in thirty minutes. A gift for devoting time and energy to not getting what I wanted is nothing to be proud of, so I don't think it's bragging to say that I became extremely good at it.

My astronomy survey course professor called me on the phone at night to talk about space and complain about his girlfriend. A news anchor texted me song lyrics while he was live on the air. I wasn't good at sports, cooking, singing, penmanship, or decorating. But I could look at a man in a way that made him drop his papers.

If fandom involves the fantasy that someone speaking to millions of people is actually just talking to you, that sense of specialness is also the gift of a crush: a hand held under a table, a look exchanged at a party, made more sublime by the excruciating pleasure of not letting it go any further.

This was true when I was single and truer when I met, in my senior year of college, the man who would become my husband. I felt lucky to have found Paul, a basketball forward who found time both to record his own music and to make sculptures in the school's pottery studio. With the sturdy good looks of the clean-cut former athlete who still goes running twice a week, he'd always been confident enough to find my crushes charming rather than a threat. And so I could enjoy other men's attention and still avoid betrayal.

"You've got a Lamborghini engine for flirting," he said. After I'd chatted at a party with a friend of his, Paul looked at me with admiration. "Jesus, what did you do to him? He never talks. But with you, suddenly he's a Civil War general, all"—in a thick Southern accent—"'Well, I declare, milady! Might I have the great privilege of accompanying ye to the Orange Blossom Cotillion?'"

I'm not saying I'm physically attractive; let's get that out of the way right now. Because that's another important lesson of womanhood: never act like you think you're hot. Appearance and seduction are unrelated anyway. Plenty of stunning people can't flirt; supposedly ugly people seduce the world all the time. When it comes to sex appeal, confidence trumps looks. Maybe models rule Hollywood, but the rest of the world belongs to the self-assured and medium pretty.

For a long time, flirting made me feel more curious and excited and ambitious—engaged, interested, available for friendship. I felt seen in new ways. Portals opened to other worlds and new playlists. Sometimes it was a tightrope act—keeping crushes from becoming serious, harnessing the heat they provided without becoming consumed by it. But I had done my ten thousand hours of practice and was an expert.

This skill served me well as a reporter and then as a ghostwriter. I also wrote books under my own name, some of which sold well enough to warrant book tours but not quite well enough to let me afford nice furniture. The main thing I'd learned from my day job: People like being asked questions. That was most of what I did all day, interviewing people. When occasionally interviewed myself, I'd try to turn inquiries back on the questioner so that by the end I'd know as much about them as they did about me.

There's a song from 1978 called "Another Girl, Another Planet." On one book tour I listened to that song every day. I thought of myself as a clutch baseball player, with that song as my walk-up music. Originally by The Only Ones but covered often, including by my favorite band, the Replacements, the song is probably about heroin— all songs from 1978 are about heroin—but I like to think it's about crushes too: "You get under my skin / I don't find it irritating."

Years ago, I pitched a book on the cultural history of the crush. No editor wanted it, despite my calling it a "cultural history," which at the time felt like a publishing skeleton key. Bookstore tables teemed with cultural histories—of crying, cheese, military formations, salt. But everyone I pitched said the same thing: *Are you insane? Crushes break your heart! They're dangerous, destabilizing, weird!*

I said they must be doing it wrong. Crushes were how you stayed a little bit in love with the world even though you had a husband. They let you sort of have more than one man without society condemning you. They let berries break upon your tongue even when you had no berries. And how safe a feeling it was inside one relationship to imagine other men stacked around protectively, like sandbags. By cultivating a deep bench of break-glass-in-case-of-emergency suitors, I was prepared for romantic disaster, just as I stayed primed to administer aid by re-upping my Red Cross certification every two years and carrying Narcan.

I could feel longing, feel it *hard*, without believing there were implications. I scoffed at people who were led around by their feelings like leashed dogs. And I did not feel deprived, or mourn what I lacked. In my fantasies, as long as those other people stayed in my head, I could be voracious while remaining faithful. I wasn't the kind of person who cheated, so only this shadowland was available, and it was enough.

I felt lucky that unlike so many of my friends, I was still sleeping with my husband. We'd always been compatible in that way if not so much in terms of kissing. Our spark came instead from bantering that quickly led to sex so technically proficient it was semiprofessional. What little compatibility we had in terms of foreplay faded over time. We didn't make out at all anymore and just cut to what we did do well. Only occasionally did "The Shoop Shoop Song (It's in His Kiss)" make me nervous.

I made certain sacrifices for my relationship, as everyone does. Paul wanted to live a creative life, which had at various times meant sculpting with clay, playing guitar, and painting. To make space for his life as an artist he had never pursued a career, though he DJ'd and helped out with friends' plays, and sometimes bartended.

He also didn't want more children once we had our son, Nate. And so I gave up on my desire to have a big family. In this, too, I found ways to enjoy what I didn't have. I spent time with other people's children. I gave them presents at the holidays and kept toys for them at my house. I took them to museums. I taught them how to sew. I read them Nate's old books.

Supporting the family kept me in a state of endless work and occasional panic. But I respected Paul for never giving up on his many artistic talents as so many friends of ours had. I was sure that one day financial success would follow. And worth more to me than any amount of money was the knowledge that my husband was a kind, loving father to our now teenage son. What was a more valuable contribution than that?

I had charming friends—a few dating back to childhood, some with whom I'd done early parenthood time at the local playground, at least a coworker or two retained from every job I'd ever had, a handful I'd only see a couple of times a year who nevertheless felt like siblings—plus some surprising ones, like Tom Hanks, who had mailed me a typewritten note about a book of mine and with whom I'd then stayed in touch.

He was considered "nice," but he was so much more than nice. He was always enthusing over a book or a radio station or a midsize industrial town, and no matter the topic he managed to come across as extremely, sharply funny; he epitomized Ralph Waldo Emerson's line, "Goodness must have some edge to it."

Paul and Nate teased me for how happy I was when these letters arrived.

"Something came in the mail from your *boyfriend*," Paul would say.

"You mean Mom's close personal friend, national treasure Tom Hanks?" Nate would reply.

They'd laugh as I took the letter into the next room to open alone.

My best and oldest friend, Veronica, who'd given up her punk band for a career as a therapist and to become the mother of two girls, said that perhaps my famous-author father's lack of interest in me had created a "Tom Hanks–size hole," adding that it was a little on the nose to compensate for a neglectful parent by becoming pen pals with someone magazines had called "America's dad."

But he wasn't a paternal figure. He was an inspiration,

like the poet W. H. Auden. I particularly loved that Auden had married Thomas Mann's daughter Erika, who like Auden was gay, to help her get a British passport and save her from the Nazis. More easily emulated: his habit of serving martinis in jam jars.

I also admired the women in my family for how they'd found meaning in caretaking and made their husbands' work possible. Denying yourself certain pleasures for the good of the whole had a quiet grace. I, too, would enjoy the satisfaction of doing the right thing, taking the high road, embodying the end of *Middlemarch*: "The growing good of the world is partly dependent on unhistoric acts; and that things are not so ill with you and me as they might have been, is half owing to the number who lived faithfully a hidden life, and rest in unvisited tombs."

In the final years of my grandmother's life I brought her books at the nursing home. She was usually doing word puzzles when I arrived. At her funeral, everyone talked about what a great marriage my grandparents had enjoyed, how she'd gotten so much fulfillment from being a wife and mother. She'd turned her early dreams of becoming a writer into domestic offerings, like long holiday letters. She was a shining example of womanhood. Sixty years of marriage. Six children. What was love if not that?

My mother, too, spoke often of the value of a long marriage. She and my father had been married several decades, though it looked like this might be their last year together.

At eighty, with terminal cancer, my father took Xanax for anxiety and Ritalin for concentration and Celexa for depression and OxyContin for pain and codeine syrup for his cough, and extra of all of them, as far as I could tell, for fun.

In spite of how many hours I spent on his care, I couldn't seem to keep him safe or make him well. There were trips to the emergency room, two car accidents, countless falls. He'd go down to 117 pounds and we'd think, *This is it!* then he'd be back up to 130. My mother began to joke that it was like in Gilbert and Sullivan's *The Pirates of Penzance*, when the police sing, over and over, "We go, we go. Yes, forward on the foe!" and after a good bit of this, the general observes, "Yes, but you *don't* go."

As he continued on in what he called "extra innings" and his doctor called "sudden death overtime," I tried to make him happy. I held weekly movie nights where my father ate big bowls of popcorn and boxes of Dots. I fixed his printer five thousand times. And yet he resisted—with impressive thoroughness—my efforts to provide us a happy ending in which he was nicer to me.

As we walked out of a hospital one day after he'd had some tests, I saw a friend's popular novel displayed in the lobby bookstore. Seeing friends' books in the wild always thrills me. It's like literary birding. I stopped to take a picture of it to send her. My father muttered, "My book's never there," indignant that his critically acclaimed modernist tomes were not nestled in among the teddy bears and "Get Well!" balloons.

We stepped out onto the street. He lit a cigarette.

"So, I'm cured!" he said as he walked to the car.

"The doctor said you're not cured," I said, "just that there's not as much of a limit now on how long you could live."

He ignored me.

My role at home as the one who listens prepared me well for ghostwriting. Most of the time I loved the work, enjoyed being the "writer" behind the "author." Though once on a late-night show I saw a celebrity who'd made my life difficult—vanishing for months and at one point dropping out so completely that the contract had almost been canceled—say: "Writing this book was hard work."

"Hard for *someone*," I said. As far as I could tell from the rest of the interview, the author still hadn't read the book.

A friend once said, as if staging an intervention with a

drunk, "I think your 'ghostwriting' identity betrays one of the big problems of translation as part of the publishing industry. You are written out of the book's presentation, marketing, and even ultimate reception, despite the fact that it's your interpretation that is dripping on every page!"

It took me a minute to realize that he pitied me. People often do. They think I'm being denied credit, that if we were in *Singin' in the Rain* I'd be sincere Kathy Selden singing for classless, flashy Lina Lamont. It's not like that. In that movie I'd be Donald O'Connor, getting the work done, whistling my way off the stage set after the scene wrapped. Or maybe one of the actors' voice coaches.

Ghostwriting is an invitation to let someone else live in your head for a while. You're a vessel through which their book passes; a surrogate, a medium. If a book is a baby, I'm the midwife, not the mother. And I was happy in the role, truly satisfied letting other people take credit. It was their story; I was just helping tell it.

The only thing I loved more than books was children. Every holiday I made sure our apartment door was decorated. I smiled when I heard a little girl greet the Halloween decorations on the way to and from school: "Hello, witch cat!" "Goodbye, witch cat!" It reminded me of when I took Nate to preschool each day and he affectionately chatted to the sharks on our neighbors' wrought-iron stoop railings, telling them what a nice day he hoped they were having.

My life was full of love. I felt fortunate. The secret of having a good life, I decided, was to live a good life.

So what was the problem?

"Sometimes, I feel like you're *too* good," said Paul one morning as he was making coffee. "It makes me feel bad. You could be a lot more selfish and I wouldn't mind. I might actually enjoy it." He said this flirtatiously, but seriously too. He seemed to have some sort of plan.

"What kind of selfishness or badness do you have in mind?" I asked, taking the cup he handed me and still not sure if he was joking.

"I know you love kissing," he said. "And I know that's never really been our thing. What if I said I'd be okay with you kissing other men?"

"What, like an open marriage?" I said. "That's insane. No. I'm fine without that."

"But what if I might even *enjoy* if you did that?" he said, monitoring my face closely for a reaction. "I mean, I like watching you flirt. Maybe you could go a bit further and I'd like it even more."

I was shocked. In my unhistoric service—as helpmeet to my parents, breadwinner in my household, ghostwriter to the stars, champion sublimator of desire—I had never thought seriously about how it might feel to kiss someone new again.

What Paul was proposing wasn't exactly an open marriage, or even PG-13, but he was opening the door a crack, while insisting the adventure would be good for me and good for us. He surely knew that only this formulation of such an exploration would have appealed to me: I could still be "good" even while being "bad."

I said I'd consider it. Then I actually did. And that is when the trouble started.

TWO

Mornington Crescent

While it was true that I never complained about how much I was doing to keep food in the house and money in the bank, it was also true that I was exhausted. For my entire adult life I'd been working more than full time while cooking, cleaning, and handling all the chores that come with responsible adulthood. If I'd been approached by the devil at a crossroads, I would have asked for nothing more than a week alone with no errands.

And so with a half-baked idea for a book project about a Victorian novelist named Ouida, I applied to do research at the British Library. I booked a trip for a week to go to London and to the novelist's hometown, then told the few people I knew in the UK that I'd be there.

Boarding the plane, I felt like I imagined my friends did leaving for summer camp. (Instead of going to camp, I'd spent childhood summers watching approximately as much television as there were hours in the day.) Paul, Nate, and my parents appeared unfazed by my departure, evidence that perhaps I was not holding my finger in the dam as much as I thought.

When I landed, I left my bags in my tiny room at a cheap, oddly shaped scholars' hotel near the British Museum and started walking around the city. Block by block, I felt my soul return to my body.

The next morning, I began my research. Given that travel and books were two of my two favorite things, being in a library in a foreign country was joy squared. And the British Library is the library-est library. I loved the efficient request desks and carrels, the luxuriously padded trays for transporting various kinds of material, and the bossy yellow signs: NO PHOTOGRAPHY ALLOWED.

You could take photos though; you just had to request permission. When I asked, a librarian came and stood over my shoulder and watched as I photographed the pages of a crumbling newspaper obituary like she was my second in a duel, my henchman, my liege. When she left my side after several minutes, I wanted to salute her.

Doing research in that library was like worshipping in

a church. For two days I flipped through Ouida's archive. She wrote in purple ink on purple paper, and in purple prose, her giant signature filling up half a sheet:

"Do you know Lady P? I do. She is an old painted yellow-haired Jewess, and she has just joined the women's Primrose Rifle Club!"

"What think you of the *régime* of vanilla cream, cayenne pepper, and unlimited brandy on which the British nation is now habitually fed?"

"I am amazed you do not see how useful to Europe it would have been to divide the USA. And it would have been even better for the Yankees. It would have prevented spreadeaglism."

Vain, petty, florid—it didn't take me long to realize she might not be someone I wanted to spend an extended period of time with, even before I got to her opinion of Tolstoy ("absolutely silly . . . I cannot think a man who believes in Christianity is a man of great intellect, and his logic is sadly defective in many other ways") and her casual prejudice ("You cannot trust Italians out of sight"). But if you go looking for anything you always find something. Research pays off even if for a while it's not obvious how.

In the archival material about her, I found other people

whose voices spoke directly into my ear. Henry James called her "unpleasant little Ouida . . . withal of a most uppish, and dauntless little spirit of arrogance and independence." Oscar Wilde corresponded with her. His letters sparkled across the years with wit and good humor. I felt love for him. I wanted to write back.

After several hours of this, I'd roam around the city and either I'd take myself out or eat with a friend. All food tasted delicious. I suddenly loved beer. I walked twenty thousand steps a day, wore dresses instead of jeans, and scribbled notes on scraps of paper. I was in love with the world and felt like it was in love with me. I wanted to kiss everyone I saw. I wouldn't, probably, but now who knew?

I met up with Ryan, an old friend who I'd worked with at one of my first jobs. I hadn't seen him much since he went to L.A. to try to become an actor and then wound up moving to the UK for a job in finance. At the pub he showed me where to sit to see all the action and what to order and how. In describing his hard-charging colleagues at work he made me laugh so hard I choked. Everything he said struck me as uniquely brilliant. I could have listened to him talk all night.

When I took a weekend trip alone to my research subject's hometown outside London, I texted Ryan throughout the trip. He charmed me by phone as he had in person. From the train there I sent him a picture of a mysterious structure covered in tubes that caught my eye out the window.

"What's this?" I asked.

"Oh, that? That's just the Martian Embassy," he said.

It was the ArcelorMittal Orbit, a sculpture and observation tower in Queen Elizabeth Olympic Park.

He turned me on to Mornington Crescent, a BBC radio game in which players engage in a battle of wits naming Tube stations, trying to get to the Mornington Crescent stop.

"King's Cross."

"Devilish move. I'll need to counter with . . . Piccadilly Circus."

"Ah! Well played. Camden."

"You've left me wide open there—Mornington Crescent!"

Everything about this game I found extremely funny, especially when the players grew indignant: "If we're not going to follow the rules, there's no point playing." There were no rules. The game was improvised. I thought it was the cleverest thing I'd ever heard of.

Ryan liked me too. He called me beguiling, told me if

I was single he'd try to marry me. Then he asked me if this was part of my research trip—if *he* might be research. I didn't say no.

On my last night in town, we ate French fries and drank beer until our other friends fell away, hour by hour, until it was just the two of us, alone at a bar, sitting very close together. He looked at me in the bar light, the rest of the crowd bustling around like porters in a train station. All was still until he leaned over and put his hand lightly on the back of my neck and pulled me toward him.

My brain shut down. His mouth tasted like beer and salty popcorn. I felt like I had as a teenager, learning what felt good and what felt even better. His body pressed against mine, and I thought, *Yes! This! I want this!*

Last call. I caught a glimpse of myself in the window, smudged makeup, hair mussed. I looked like someone completely different, someone rumpled and fascinating. We left it at that because that was enough. I tried to figure out what the name was for the feeling I got from that kiss—and the other side of the same precious coin: the freedom to wander around a strange city. It was something like *power*, or openness to adventure. And I must have been radiating it because everyone seemed to want to talk to me. That whole trip, if I sat down alone in a pub for dinner, within minutes a man would ask if the seat next to me was taken.

Whenever Ryan had gotten up to get us another drink, he'd returned to find someone talking to me. A disproportionate number of these men were named Sean, so Ryan started to tease me about having ensorcelled a nation of Seans. I felt like I was in a game show money booth with bills flying all around me, only instead of money, the currency was attention. I could have as much as I could grab.

And kissing Ryan wasn't really *cheating*. If anything, it was just a slight *veering*. I looked at the Underground map and felt that I was not so far afield of the Central Zone. I imagined myself still just in Zone 2, safe.

Why had I denied myself for so long? And why were so many tales about women's sexuality so depressing? "Sexy" people had always reminded me of the Texas expression "all hat, no cattle"—a cowboy who doesn't actually have a ranch, just the outfits.

But in London I was *truly* sexy. My secret had nothing to do with fashion or technique or anything taught by women's magazines; it was joy. The discovery felt mythological, like a sword pulled from a stone, an herb stolen from a garden. Suddenly it felt good to sleep and good to wake up. It felt good to be tired and good to be working. Blankets felt good, and wind. Bad things felt good. Good things felt like heaven.

I once heard about a scholar who, as she was sitting down on the dais at an academic conference, looked to her left and her right and said, "Ah, it's wonderful when you've slept with everyone on your panel." I thought of the bumper sticker GOOD GIRLS GO TO HEAVEN—BAD GIRLS GO EVERYWHERE, and felt its truth. I was only being a little bad, and I already felt happier than I had in years.

While still in London, I had tea with an old ex-boyfriend and his new partner. I thought of the Taylor Swift line in "Invisible String" about how she used to grind a cold axe for her exes and now she buys their babies presents. I bought his baby a Petit Bateau onesie, and we had a lovely afternoon.

I felt at peace now with all the men who'd ever rejected me, like a bookish friend I was obsessed with when I was nineteen. He made me read so much George Steiner. I got through all of *After Babel* and he still wouldn't date me; I wanted to take him to court. But I'd since become the very pink of forgiveness. I genuinely wished him—

wished everyone—well. And the world kept rewarding me for my magnanimity.

At an outdoor café on a street lined with expensive clothing stores, I had drinks with a dashing friend at which he said—and if I hadn't heard something similar from a bunch of Seans that week I'd have been caught off guard—that he found me attractive. I liked how he smiled with his whole face and how he used dramatic flourishes to make his points.

"You're making me blush," I said. "I'm glad I have makeup on so you can't tell."

"I can tell," he said.

We left it at that. But that was plenty. Until that trip it had been a long time since I'd had a sense of freedom, possibility, and being at home in the world—not as a mother, wife, and daughter, but as someone new in town, someone who sort of enjoyed getting lost on the Underground.

When I got an NHS alert that I'd been exposed to COVID, Ryan said he was glad because if I was positive he probably was too. That meant we could quarantine together at his apartment and stay in bed for ten days.

"I've never wished so hard for someone to have COVID," he said.

The test was negative.

While I walked around London, I called Veronica and asked her why as a happily married woman in middle age I'd become, all of a sudden, some sort of vixen.

"Because you're *alive*," she said.

That was how I felt: more alive than I'd felt in a long time. The more alive I felt, the more attention I got, and the more alive I became, on and on in an endless cycle of aliveness. I walked down the street convinced that I was glowing.

I'd only felt even close to that radiant once before. After high school, using my babysitting money, I spent months backpacking, walking for hours through one city or another. When I was hungry I stopped at a bakery and got a hunk of bread. When I was tired I lay down on a hostel bed. When I craved company I sat in a park and hoped whoever talked to me wasn't a murderer.

Having been raised agnostic, in those days I was what hippies call a seeker. I craved a connection to the eternal, an undeniable encounter with the ineffable. *Something* was calling me, but I couldn't name what it was. I thought perhaps I was looking for someone or something to love with my whole heart. Whether that meant religion or romantic love, surely God or men would take me out of myself; either one would do.

Over the years, my craving for a mystical experience

passed away like my penchant for clove cigarettes. Like all my friends not in the middle of an active crisis, I had settled into something that looked a lot like contentment.

Veronica, too, had built so much for herself. We talked on the phone all the time about how big our lives were, how lucky we felt. She and I had friends, spouses, children, jobs, volunteer work. How could we be disappointed when we'd received so much?

Generations of women had struggled to "have it all," and here I was now, the final panel in the evolution chart. Since London, I'd been listening on repeat to Lucinda Williams's "Passionate Kisses" and Mary Chapin Carpenter's "I Take My Chances." In considering women's problems, I'd begun to wonder if we weren't aiming too high, expecting too much, but rather aiming *far too low.* Freedom and security could be compatible! Why not?

My marriage was a road stretching all the way to the horizon. I could take little detours off that main avenue, onto the side streets of other men, as long as none of the detours became its own road. Only sometimes did I worry that all the energy I put into crushes could be better spent. But I had faith in my ability to control them. And the risk was paying off.

In London, I couldn't stop thinking of how I'd been as a teenager. I could vividly recall how it felt to drink a light and sweet coffee at lunch on a fall day in front of my high school. I floated back to class smelling like coffee and oranges and smoke and fresh air and Herbal Essences shampoo, a pencil in my ponytail, my bra strap showing.

"When we're young we're so open to the world," Veronica said on the phone as I talked to her while walking through the city. In the background, I could hear her girls watching a movie and laughing. "And you're like that now. So maybe that's why you're thinking about your teen years again."

Back then, I'd spent time with a classmate on stoops and rooftops, enjoying a classic 1990s no-labels-friendship-but-we-slept-together. As adults, we ate salad on lunch breaks from his lawyer job. One day he said he was thinking of switching careers, and he'd found himself thinking back to a night in my twin bed after the prom. While rolling around, we'd accidentally broken one of the commemorative glasses they gave us.

"Oh! Should we stop and clean that up?" he'd said.

"Do you want to?" I'd asked.

He said that prom night was one of the only times he

vividly remembered being asked what he wanted. And so he found himself thinking of that now and asking himself—as he'd asked himself whether he wanted to be a good kid and immediately clean up broken glass or continue to fool around with his non-girlfriend girlfriend— whether he wanted to keep being a lawyer or go back to school for something more fun.

What was the takeaway? That sex with me in the 1990s was better than sweeping up broken glass. And also that there's power in asking earnest questions about what we want, especially when it's a more difficult choice than sex versus vacuuming.

I wanted to send word to my generational cohort: *Don't we make our own cages? When we rattle the bars don't we often find that they are made of cardboard? That we've cut them out for ourselves with X-ACTO knives? Look! We are free! We have nothing to lose but our PTA membership!*

In *The Notes,* Ludwig Hohl advised: "Work toward raising the emotional state of one's usual (daily) life to the state one is in when *traveling*—to that state of openness, of readiness to offer oneself, of being able to see things in their full proportion, of internal tension and fecundity of thought—*that* is life."

London had given me this elevated emotional state. I

felt like a new person—or like my true self, like Bette Davis at the end of *Now, Voyager*, a siren emerging from beneath layers of split ends and line-toeing. I'd walked for miles and kissed a man deeply for the first time in many years. Then it was time to go home.

THREE

Bad Now

Transitioning from vacation, you have to pay the credit card bill. The car you took to the beach is full of sand. Your sunburn starts to peel. I anticipated fallout from my adventuring, but there was almost none.

"I kissed Ryan," I told Paul as soon as we were alone.

"What? Really?" he said. "I was wondering why you seemed so cheerful."

"You're not mad?"

"No, I think it's great! I love the new you! Tell me everything."

To Paul, my kissing Ryan was just a more intense version of the flirtation with other men that he liked. He enjoyed being with someone who other men desired, to see his wife flush with aliveness. He said he felt like I'd lost my sparkle. He'd feared it was gone for good, but now it was back.

When he and I met in college, we'd fallen in love fast. And then we'd never once seriously considered breaking up. He always said that he knew early on that he wanted to be with me forever, in part because he knew he'd never get bored. He praised me for being good company. I helped reconcile him to his family. His father had died a year before I went to London; when I went to clean out his apartment I was touched by all the photos of me he'd hung on his wall.

"You'd never gotten attention like that before you met Paul," Veronica said. "He's always been so into you. You knew he wasn't going anywhere."

I liked being married. I marveled at how that ceremony cast a spell, turned me into a new person, a *wife*. Then we had a child! Even more to bind us. I had holiday cards on the fridge and a ring on my finger. And having Nate had made me more ambitious. I wanted to make my family rich and strong and healthy, just as I'd fattened my baby by nursing him until he lolled back, milk dribbling down his chin as he slept.

With that baby now practically an adult, Paul and I often went out for a nice dinner and then had what we agreed was quite good sex for people our age.

I still liked him so much. I was sure I'd been hard to be around plenty of times for many reasons, but he kindly did not talk much about that, an omission more to his credit than mine. Yes, we had other problems, and they boiled down—as they do in so many marriages—to sex and money.

The sex part: he'd had an affair with a friend of his named Sarah when Nate was little. Well, not a *real* affair. They'd fallen for each other, which was rough enough. But Paul had told me before anything physical happened between them, and said he would give her up for me. They'd stopped hanging out. He felt a lot of guilt, but I'd reassured him that it was okay. He'd behaved well. I was proud of us for being open and honest with each other even about the hardest things.

The money part: I'd been asking him for almost as long as we'd been together to find some way to earn money aside from occasional gigs. I found supporting us stressful. But for whatever reason, I had a talent for hustling that he lacked.

The issue would come up every six months, and we'd have a long, hard conversation.

"You knew I wasn't a stockbroker when you married me," he would say. "You liked that I was this way."

"Yes," I'd reply, "but now we have a child. We need more money coming in."

"I'd be happy to live on less," he would say. "And the only way I'll ever make money from my art is if I fully devote myself to it. Or have you lost faith in me?"

That would be the end of it. If I wanted to live on more than an artist's income, that was for me to figure out. And so I'd compromised on that the same way I'd given in on not having more children even though I'd always wanted three.

I'd complain to Veronica on the phone, talk about the pressure of debt and how it meant I had to suspend my own creative work. Often I wished I was constitutionally able to live more like Paul did, with a low-stakes part-time day job. She'd say that I had two choices: I could leave him or suck it up. I chose the latter, year after year, because it seemed like a small price to pay for a companionable marriage. We were on the same team, and each other's biggest fan. When I traveled, Paul took care of Nate, fed the cat, cleaned.

My mother was impressed, she said, that I'd built a life where I could have so much, with a man who even cooked. She had been undermined at many points in her life, given up on various dreams because she lacked support. When she was young she studied ballet. She was so good that one of the best ballerinas in the world wanted my mother to be the little girl opposite her in *The Nutcracker*. But her parents said no; they didn't want to take her to that many rehearsals and give up their Christmas vacation. She begged to be allowed to fulfill what she saw as her destiny. They still said no.

In my estimation, my father didn't properly respect her dreams either. She'd tried to travel for work when I was little, but when she was away he didn't watch me closely. Before and after school I walked alone through lower Manhattan, even though a little boy three years older than me had vanished nearby not long before and was presumed dead. My father said he couldn't do more; he had writing to do. My mother stopped traveling so much. At parties with her husband's intellectual colleagues my mother held her own but felt, in her high heels and thick mascara, like *Gone with the Wind*'s brothel madam Belle Watling flouncing into a Roz Chast cartoon.

He said she didn't have creative ambition in the same way he did, and so it made sense that more space was made for his work. He doubted my seriousness too.

Drowning in my day job and freelance work when Nate

was a tiny baby, I told him that Veronica had given me good advice: "Three words: Lower. The. Bar."

"Well, I could never do that," he said. "I have standards."

He looked down on me for ghostwriting, and for agreeing to publicity when my books came out. When I told him about interviews I was doing, thinking he'd be proud, he said, "Promotion *uber alles*, huh?"

I was already living a life my mother and grandmother never could. And now on top of all that I was being allowed—encouraged even—to kiss people. As one relationship after another had imploded around us and many had ended over affairs, Paul and I had endured. We felt sorry for other people who didn't have what we did.

One night as I folded clothes in the living room, I told Paul that maybe he'd been right: I could be a bit more like Ado Annie in *Oklahoma*, for which I'd served on the tech crew in middle school. She sang the promiscuity anthem "I Cain't Say No." What an inspiration! Where was the harm in Ado Annie's failure to say "nix" to farmhands making passes at her?

I said I was feeling weirdly alive since London.

"You're bad now!" Paul said, sounding proud. "I think this feels mystical because it's your identity. You're feeling free and seen and embodied the way young people do when they come out. This is who you are and you're finally admitting it."

He wondered if this could be the start of something even more ambitious. He thought perhaps we could start by reading the polyamory book *Polysecure*. He thought being more open might help us lead more exciting and more actualized lives, both as individuals and as a couple. And he thought it would be hot.

The idea didn't particularly turn me on. Still, I did like how I felt in London, and there had been no negative fallout from the trip. If the question was should I stay married to Paul or kiss a friend every once in a while, then obviously I'd choose marriage. But if the question was if I'd like to do both with no consequences other than radiating this new sexual energy, the answer was equally obvious.

"Men like that give themselves a lot of *permission*," my mother once said of someone we knew who had affairs.

Yes, that's right—permission is gross, I'd thought at the time. Asking for what you wanted, doing what you pleased— in spite of the indulgent language around self-care, a surprising amount of shame and resistance still showed up when we started to ask, even a little, *No, really, what do I want and why don't I do it?*

Now, though, I wondered why permission was so bad.

There were a number of well-written, thoughtful articles just then swirling around online about negotiating open marriages. They didn't make it sound ideal; in some cases, it seemed transactional. I couldn't help thinking that it meant getting out in front of one potential problem—the danger of illicit extramarital sex—by creating a new problem: the emotional and logistical complexity of licit extramarital sex.

Was the idea of an open marriage traditionally more appealing to men than women because of some kind of back-brain insecurity women had by virtue of facing more consequences from pregnancy than men? Indoctrination into fairy-tale fantasies about exclusive soulmate romance? Or could it be that, even in the age of reliable birth control, we hadn't let ourselves desire more? Postpandemic, the time felt right for radical thinking: *Did we want to go back to an office? Was living in a city still important?* If all the usual rules had gone out the window, what if sexually, too, we just . . . did what we wanted?

I'd always liked books by drunk older male writers, and I finally realized why: By eight thirty in the morning I'd fed my child and gotten him off to school, listened to the news, done a load of laundry, answered a dozen emails, edited a stack of pages—and by two p.m. a Harry Crews character had drunk two beers and checked on his captured bird of prey. Who needed fantasy novels when there existed such exotic tales of dissipation?

Nate saw me reading Harry Crews's *The Hawk Is Dying* while drinking coffee one morning.

"I just saw a falconry demonstration online," he said. "Want to see?"

I did.

He brought his phone over. On his screen, a beautiful bird launched off his keeper's gauntlet. The announcer said, "The bird will hunt now and bring back its catch." The people watched as the bird flew away from the falconer's hand, up, up into the clouds. It snatched a pigeon out of the sky . . . and kept on flying. For an uncomfortably long period of time the crowd stared into the sky waiting for the bird to bring the pigeon back to his fleece-wearing handler.

Eventually, they stopped looking up and turned quizzically toward one another as the trainer continued to squint at the clouds.

I burst out laughing. "It just kept going?" I said.

"Yes!" said Nate with glee. We watched several more times, trying to pinpoint the exact second that the falconer realized the falcon wouldn't be coming back.

FOUR

The Reading

I dreamed about the British Library—the mezzanine coffee shop, the thick plastic bags for carrying PEN-CILS ONLY into the Reading Room, the candy-colored lockers. Full of longing for who I was there and how free I felt, I started to make plans to see friends and to work on projects and to look around for other men I could flirt with and perhaps even kiss.

In the course of this campaign, I reached out to David, a handsome friend from college with whom I'd happily have been locked in a closet. If Paul and I hadn't started dating then, I might have pursued David. And yet, I wasn't sure he'd have been interested. As long as I'd known him, he'd preferred reading to parties. He was quiet, but when he spoke people leaned in to listen. I had a low-key crush on him for years. How could you not? He was at once bookish and smoldering. I'd have made him with a computer like those guys made Kelly Le-Brock in *Weird Science*.

When I looked him up for the first time in a while, I could see that he'd grown nerdier, with thick glasses and clothes that somehow always seemed askew. Yet he still had an undeniable appeal, with strong arms and kind eyes. At the prestigious university several states away where he taught religion, he was a favorite professor—buoyant, disheveled, disarmingly earnest. Somehow he'd avoided the anti-sincere drubbing of our generation; he must have hopped back onto the curb as that bus hit everyone else.

It had been years since we'd last been in touch, but when I texted, he replied eight minutes later.

"I've almost written you several times," he said. "I read your last book!"

"So you're the one," I said.

"I loved it. Really. I'm heading into class right now, but I'd been meaning to tell you what your work meant to me. Now I will!"

Two hours later, a long email arrived. He delivered a gorgeously written review in which he said something I found profound. He said he thought the book was partly about the damage done by bohemians who didn't revolt enough against the values with which they'd been raised. When David rebelled against his unrepentant hippie parents, he'd constructed a new value system from the ground up by reading widely. Even in college, he didn't do drugs or sleep around. He believed in the virtue of solitude to an extreme that girlfriends had found alienating.

He told me that he'd recently discovered that his nickname around campus was the Monk, but he didn't mind. Better, he thought, to have a reputation as uptight than as a libertine. And though conscientious, he was not a prig. Every rule he followed was one he negotiated with his own conscience. When you leave a tradition, as he had eschewed his parents' hedonism, it's important to replace what you reject with something better, he said. Otherwise why bother?

This unconventionality seemed promising for my designs on him. But he scorned the bed-hopping of his academic colleagues. When women came on to him—and I suspected many did because he looked like Indiana Jones in the campus scenes before he became an adventurer— I bet he talked to them about pleasures of the flesh versus of eternity until they turned around and started talking to someone more likely to put out.

He said more about my writing—so much more, including praise so specific and generous that it felt like I'd just been photographed with a camera somehow at once high definition and infinitely forgiving. In his rave I thought I saw a blurring of his affection for the work and for me.

It can be hard to separate how we feel about people from how we feel about what they make. That's why Veronica said she'd been burned one too many times by blurbs heralding books as unputdownable when she'd found them to be, in fact, quite putdownable. She said there should be stickers on books: "No sexual favors were provided in exchange for these blurbs." (When I told that to my editor friend Helen, she said, "No! The blurb industry would collapse!")

I wrote a long email back to David. He replied swiftly with one equally long. We were both showing off, making each other laugh. Our enthusiasm picked up speed like a boulder rolling down a hill. Within a week, we were checking in with each other several times a day. Soon David started to tell me about his students, his family, and his research, saying each time, "I don't do this. I don't talk about myself." He said that for a long time he'd found it difficult even to get up in front of his classes.

I, on the other hand, a dutiful book-tourer, had a lot of experience talking about myself; and I enjoyed asking questions and hearing what he had to say. Every time another message from him landed I felt as though I'd been handed a small, perfect gift. And all I had to do to get more was ask. I kept putting quarters in the slot machine throughout the day; every pull yielded a jackpot.

Pulling myself away from the computer was difficult once I started composing a reply. But one evening I had to because, for the first time since the upheaval of the pandemic, I was asked to do a reading. It was part of a series held by a cheerful, community-minded young man on a kayak pier.

Paul came with me. We left Nate alone with takeout. As the sun set, I sipped a plastic cup of red wine and watched kayakers dart across the water like bugs skimming the surface. We watched the rain hold off until it didn't, and the event moved to a lounge located inside the kayak rental shop.

A comedian and a musician performed, and then I did my reading. During the Q&A that followed, people asked deep questions and laughed at my jokes. I said that I wrote and read to feel less alone.

"Rilke said that books are like a sealed envelope passed to the future," I said. "People sometimes think writing and reading are solitary acts. But both can be a way to see and be seen more clearly. The children's book author Kate DiCamillo says that the notebook she carries around is a reminder to "pay attention; pay attention; pay attention."

I gestured to the crowd—some old people, someone

holding a new baby, a few smartly dressed people on dates. Being together like that, just a group of human beings in a room, felt important whether I was the one talking or the one listening.

I said that I'd long wondered if going many years without publishing anything had been, as so many key choices in life are, an elaborate revenge scheme. An art teacher I had in middle school said you weren't a real artist unless you shared what you made. I protested. I was writing a lot that I wasn't sharing. I did not want to be told by a community theater director in architect glasses that therefore my work had no value. I vowed not to publish anything ever; that would show her.

What she should have said, of course, was: "Some things take time to find their way into the world. As James Salter said, 'There are stories one must tell, and years when one must tell them.' One day you'll be around people who want to hear what you have to say."

Walking home after the event was over, I turned to Paul, who seemed uncharacteristically quiet. "How'd I do?" I said.

"What?" he said, as if it were a strange question to ask. "Oh, great. But that conversation raised a lot of questions for me. I've never really found my outlet, you know?

I haven't done anywhere near all I hoped. I feel like no one cares what I have to say."

I tried to focus on him as he talked. He was fired up, and I knew that in such circumstances it was often best just to provide a sympathetic ear. He continued to talk all the way home, and as we sat on the couch, and as we lay in bed.

At one a.m. he was still talking. I considered trying to change the subject toward something light that would let us sleep, though given the heaviness of the existential angst he was describing I feared my deflection would come across as the old joke, "Otherwise, Mrs. Lincoln, how did you like the play?"

At this point I made a strategic error. I told him things weren't as bleak as he said. I pointed out all the good in his life. And I noted that he kept saying a number over and over again for how much money he made, and it wasn't right: "It's half that," I said, "but that's okay!" I went on (I should not have gone on) to say that being the sole bread-winner had been, as he knew, hard for me at times, like when Nate was a baby. I hadn't had the option to stay home with him. When I was trying to write my first real book it took years because I had to work to support us at the same time.

"But I accept that imbalance now," I said, thinking this would make him feel good, and he would be impressed with my beneficence. "I got over it. Now I don't even feel like you should do anything else. I came to realize that you deserve half of what I make because you do a lot of intangible things to help the family. And you've always been so supportive."

Sadly, his love language was not Withering Critique.

"You're making me feel worse!" he said, his forehead furrowed. "I was coming to you with my problems and you're basically saying that I should feel bad. And I know other men are into you right now. I get that you're distracted. But I want your attention too."

"The whole thing about other men was your idea!" I said, sitting up in bed, abandoning all hope of falling asleep. "I thought you liked it."

"I do!" he said. "But it's confusing. Promise you won't leave me."

"I won't leave you," I said, but he didn't seem to hear me.

That evening lasted a century. He slammed a cupboard when he got out a glass for water, and I worried that he'd wake up Nate. I told him to be quieter, which only made him more upset. Staying up all night fighting is my idea of hell; I'd list it as an allergy on health forms if I could.

As Paul wound down and I was able to close my eyes

around five in the morning, I noticed my mind drift to David. I thought of a quote he'd sent me that day from the French philosopher Paul Valéry, one of many writers it turned out we both loved: "If we are worth anything it is only because we have been, or have the power to be, 'beside ourselves' for a moment. . . . There are molecules of time which differ from the others as a grain of gunpowder differs from a grain of sand. They look much the same but their futures are quite different."

Were David and I gunpowder or sand? I wasn't sure. But I thought there might be a clue in one exchange that day. He'd said, "In spite of you trying to distract me, I graded all the exams!" I'd replied, and I realized as I lay there in bed that my reply dimmed the lights, set a record spinning on the turntable: "When I'm trying to distract you, you'll know."

FIVE

What Takes Place in the Soul

This is what takes place in the soul:—

1. Admiration.
2. A voice within says: "What pleasure to kiss, to be kissed."
3. Hope.

—Stendhal, *On Love*, 1822

When David, as chair of his department, had to deal with furious fellow academics, he did so with equanimity. The distraught or demanding could say anything, and he'd listen carefully, work to understand the message beneath the vitriol, and do what needed to be done. Describing to me how he'd recently quelled a crisis, I thought of a line from *Parks and Recreation*. Leslie Knope accepts her community members' scorn with a smile, for what were enraged town hall meeting attendees doing but "caring loudly at" her?

I was reminded of something I'd witnessed at Disney World when Nate was five. A woman ahead of us in line was trying to fight with the woman serving breakfast, but she wouldn't fight back.

"For that price, how can there be only *three* waffles?"

"Oh! Would you like more? Here, let me sneak another one onto your plate."

"Is juice not included?! This is an outrage!"

"We do have a special including juice! Would you like that? I'd be happy to get that for you!"

It was like watching someone try to scale a plexiglass wall.

I was charmed by David's unflappable good nature. How funny, I thought, that I'd reached out to him thinking I'd add him to my stable of crushes, and he'd quickly become one of my best friends. I'd thought I wanted him to like me, but it turned out I wanted to be like him. In our correspondence about books and minutiae I felt like the best version of myself.

When he mentioned that his day had been a campus nightmare like something out of Julie Schumacher's epistolary academic satire *Dear Committee Members*, I walked to the nearest bookstore, bought the book, read it in one sitting, and wrote him an email in the book's style. Any other work I had to get done that day seemed secondary to making him laugh with a letter of recommendation in the style of Schumacher's long-suffering English professor Jason Fitger.

Crushes had always made me feel powerful. This was the opposite. I was lit up, but I wasn't in control. None of my old tricks worked anymore. I was rich in a defunct currency. A trillion zloty and I couldn't buy a stick of gum.

The only consolation for my lack of agency was that David seemed mystified, too, by his own sense of powerlessness. He kept asking why he wanted to tell me so much. That wasn't a problem for me. Why *wouldn't* I tell him everything? He was the warmest audience, the most attentive interlocutor. I was charmed by his jokes and moved by his stories. If London made me feel drunk, now I felt like I'd taken a hallucinogen. Not a minute went by that I didn't wonder what he was up to. Every time I turned a corner I saw something new I wanted to tell him about.

His emails were so well crafted that I sometimes laughed at their refinement. There were footnotes and links to sources, multiple languages and their translations. He had a formality more befitting the nineteenth century. I felt myself resist it at first, but soon found that I loved the way he talked, especially the anachronisms.

I'd always tried to put my finger on an odd feeling I've had at least once every time while becoming close with a new person—a sort of *squeamishness*. The person says something, does something that you would have said bothered you, something embarrassing or silly or too sincere. Instead of rejecting the gesture and condemning them, you embrace it, think, *Maybe I do like someone who chews on their hair. Maybe I find an ironic T-shirt collection adorable.*

In *On Love*, Stendhal describes a process of "crystallization": "At the salt mines of Salzburg a branch stripped of its leaves by winter is thrown into the abandoned depths of the mine; taken out two or three months later it is covered with brilliant crystals. . . ."

In the glow of my bejeweled connection to David I felt radiantly happy just walking around. I was transported by everyday smells like the burnt-salt of fresh pretzels or the old paper of the library's reading room. I started wearing the sparkly rings I'd inherited from my grandmother, marveling at the rainbows they cast when light streamed in through the window.

"I feel like Emily in *Our Town* after she dies and realizes how precious life is, only I don't have to return to the

Grover's Corners graveyard afterward!" I told my friend
Helen over drinks. I said that very minute my inbox was
likely filling up with emails from David, and that they'd
contain the best stories I'd ever heard.

Helen seemed to be catching some kind of contact high
from what I was telling her. She asked a thousand questions, responding to every answer as though the story of
our correspondence was a concert by her favorite band.

After we paid the check and left the bar, she walked
alongside me for a few blocks. As we waited to cross the
street, she turned to me with a stupefied look on her
face—eyes dilated, lids lowered—that I'd only ever seen
in cartoons after the character ingested an aphrodisiac.
She leaned over and kissed me on the mouth.

Surprised, I kissed her back. I'd somehow never kissed
another woman before, not even in college. Her lips felt
soft and warm. Her dark hair rested on the shoulders of
her blazer. I noticed for the first time that she was extremely pretty. We made out on the street corner, then
pulled away. And then we burst out laughing.

"I don't know what that was about!" she said. "I'm sorry.
I think maybe I've been a little pent up. Something about
what you were saying made me lose my mind."

"Maybe Love Potion Number Nine is just four vodka
sodas," I said. "And I'm not complaining. That was nice."

When I got home I told Paul what had happened.

"You're hell on wheels!" he said approvingly.

Was this who I was now? I thought. I'd barely kissed at all in years and now I'd made out with two new people in a matter of weeks. It felt weird not to be in trouble when everything felt so intense.

"Whatever, the world is weird now since the pandemic," Paul said. "We're all trying to get out of our houses after being cooped up too long. It's two a.m. everywhere."

COVID had changed everything. If the world as we knew it was over, how did we want to construct the new world? Could I really have, without apology, a husband and also an openness to kissing other people, plus one unprecedented connection to a religious studies professor in another state? If anyone judged me for it, could I just not care? When Nate was in middle school and getting wrapped up in his friends' drama, every morning at drop-off I said as he went up the stairs, "I love you! Have fun! Care less!" Maybe that was good advice.

My family life was enhanced, not diminished, by whatever was happening. I made Nate food and took long walks with him, helped him with his college applications without losing patience. I tended to my parents when they needed me and was able to enjoy their company without feeling overly involved. I knew from the time in London that if I wasn't around the world didn't stop spinning. I had poker nights and a picnic club and attended readings. I had coffees and dinner and drinks with girlfriends who told me about their marriages and their projects and their children. Letters from Tom Hanks continued to arrive; Paul and Nate continued to tease me about them.

And David had become the best friendship I'd had in as long as I could remember. Somehow he'd become essential. I felt that I needed other languages to even get close to explaining it. I read a book about the Gaelic concept of *anam cara*, or "soul friend," the person with whom you could share your deepest self and feel that you completely belonged.

We didn't know quite what to do with each other except marvel. Our connection had begun to feel like a religious calling. In our correspondence I felt like I'd embarked on a pilgrimage, only with no clue where it led. In his presence I began to feel more and more like myself, but for the first time. I also felt like I'd been hugging the world hard my whole life, and now the world's arms were wrapping around me and squeezing back.

What David and I had felt sacred—the word that kept coming to mind was *important*.

Was this what being devout was like? As a child, I'd

been fascinated by the religious practices of my class-mates. Daniel went to Hebrew school each week near the pool hall. Veronica's mother set out big bowls of oranges and incense. Eleanor dressed up and went to a smoky Catholic church; when I went with her, the standing up and sitting down felt like a Hokey Pokey I couldn't get the hang of. In my teens, I spent three months alone in India, staying at dollar-a-night hostels. I got caught up in the holiday Holi and wound up laughing hysterically, covered head to toe in multicolored paint after getting socked with paint-filled water balloons.

On a trip through the Holy Land as a nanny I left my room at three in the morning to climb Mount Sinai alone. At the top, I watched the sun rise. In those moments—and many years later giving birth and nursing—I felt a sense of the holy. I always wondered how anyone could look at a tree or a baby and not believe in some sort of animating spirit beyond what we could see or prove. It seemed, more than anything else, like bad manners: *Black holes, childbirth, eagles, forgiveness— eh, I'm not convinced. What else ya got?*

As a new wife and mother, I started going to church. I learned when to stand and when to kneel and when to cross myself and when to say, "And also with you." And yet, once I'd become an adult, I'd given up on mysticism. So many of the people who talked about supernatural experiences seemed like kooks, with eyes like saucers.

My mature religious faith could be summed up by the Mister Rogers dictum, "Look for the helpers." I cried when a marathon went by my house—as a band set up on the corner played "Road Runner" over and over for hours—because I loved seeing people trying to do something difficult and onlookers telling them they could do it. They didn't *know* these sweaty strangers could do anything, much less run for twenty-six miles, but by having faith they were making it more likely that the runners would finish the race. Prayers change the person praying too—they pull you closer to your better self.

When I was writing, as a cash grab, about wicker and vaulted ceilings for *Country Living* magazine, one of the fancy-home owners and I bonded over our love of Christmas. She shared a letter with me that someone had given her when she'd bemoaned her daughter's losing faith in Santa. The letter, written by a children's book author and posted online, proposed telling the "Is Santa real?" child this:

"Santa is bigger than any person, and his work has gone on longer than any of us have lived. . . . Throughout your life, you will need this capacity to believe: in yourself, in your friends, in your talents, and in your family. You'll also need to believe in things you can't measure or even hold in your hand. Here, I am talking about love. . . . Santa is love and magic and hope and happiness. I'm on his team, and now you are, too."

How slick is *that*? You have two choices in life, kid: you can believe in Santa and get presents or you can *be* Santa and give them. No middle ground! No sitting back, skeptical and judgmental and smarter-than-gullible-little-kids. You get Santa done unto you or you do Santa unto others. I found that brilliant. And in my life I felt I'd received so much good fortune that I had an obligation to provide as much to others as possible.

But now? I'd leveled up. What I felt was beyond goodness; it was *wonder*. Within weeks of the start of our correspondence, David became, as the song goes, my favorite waste of time.

He was travel and libraries rolled into one. He surprised me every day. He introduced me to writers I'd thought I knew but had never actually read, like Ralph Waldo Emerson, who I'd had mixed up with Thoreau and filed under *something-something-alone-in-the-woods-something*. Every one of his essays seemed to be about us.

From "Friendship": "The moment we indulge our affections, the earth is metamorphosed; there is no winter, and no night; all tragedies, all ennuis, vanish,—all duties even; nothing fills the proceeding eternity but the forms all radiant of beloved persons. Let the soul be assured that somewhere in the universe it should rejoin its friend, and it would be content and cheerful alone for a thousand years."

Exactly right! Looking for explanations of how I felt about David, I jumped from one book to the other as if they were stepping stones across a river.

From *The Epistolary Flirt* from 1896:

"Irwin: And you think of me all the rest of the time?

"Evangeline: Not exactly think—that implies a voluntary action. But nearly every minute of my days and dreams has a sort of Irwinian flavor."

My days acquired a Davidian flavor, the diffuse aliveness of the prior months focusing to a point that was his email address.

We read a book about Kabbalah that talked about "a fallen spark from the World of Love."

Yes! I thought. *That's what I've caught! A spark!*

I was becoming a version of myself that I liked better than any other iteration. And if by man's law I was tempting fate by spending so much time talking to a man who wasn't my husband, by a higher power to do anything else seemed wrong. Plus, as a writer, wasn't it my job to be inspired? Here was daily inspiration! And I still had the energy to get my work done, and—electrified as I was—for sex with Paul.

I felt like a better mother too. Nate and I discussed his New Year's resolutions, getting more sleep and not procrastinating. I said I was trying to think of some that would be good for me. He said that I was perfect and didn't need to make any. *While they're young, sons probably should think their mothers are angels*, I thought. I wondered how long that would last. Because the truth—Emersonian glosses aside, and regardless of the fact that David and I hadn't touched—was that I was courting something that in pretty much every culture throughout history is a sin. To Paul and to myself I'd been saying of my correspondence with David: "It's not what it looks like!" But sometimes I thought: *What if it's exactly what it looks like?*

SIX

Elegant Things

I think about you a lot," David said on our first Zoom call, which we referred to as a staff meeting. "Like, all the time."

We'd been writing to each other every day, thousands of words by email and text. I thought about him as I fell asleep and when I woke up. But I hadn't seen him in a long time. Now he was there on my screen. We both looked dazed.

"What do you think about?" I asked.

"Things I want to tell you or show you. Things I think you'd like or that I want you to see."

Looking very serious, he asked if I understood what we were feeling. I said no and asked if he did. He said no.

We stared at each other. I thought I might die; the cause of death would be a desire to tousle his hair.

What we felt was different than anything I'd known before, more all-encompassing. So what, if anything, were we supposed to do with it? The staff meeting adjourned, as staff meetings often do, with no resolution and no action items. Later that day I went to check my mail and found a box from him containing seventeen books. I sent him a photo of them all spread out on my bed, the cat looking at them curiously.

What exactly was happening? Infatuation? Lust? I was not sure any of the things I wanted from him were possible. But what we'd had so far felt impossible too. It also felt essential. Around him, it was as if I'd gone through a wardrobe into a land full of white witches and gentle lions and Turkish Delight for every meal.

And yet, if someone had asked who he was to me, I wouldn't have known what to say. He was more than a friend but not a lover. Every time I got an email from him I thought at first that I had nothing to say in reply. Then an hour or two would pass and there we'd be again, thousands of words tying days up in ribbons.

One day David and I began—because this was the kind of thing that happened—sending each other emails in the style of the thousand-year-old Japanese court diary *The Pillow Book of Sei Shōnagon*. The form reminded me a little bit of *Family Feud* ("Things the Doctor Says," "Things You Bring Camping").

He wrote:

29. Elegant Things
The "Time Passes" section in *To the Lighthouse*. Your metaphors. "Another Girl, Another Planet." Your nails in the photos you send of your hands holding books.

102. People Who Seem to Suffer
Lovers. Saints. Authors. Academics. Bohemians.

199. The Answer Is "No"
Any question you ask that begins with "Is it bad . . . ?" Please don't stop asking, though, even though you know my answer.

I wrote:

108. Things That Are Intriguing Mysteries
How you have time to teach when you write me so much.

124. One Has Carefully Scented a Robe
I'm glad you like my manicures. One of the things that made me start doing that was embracing the song "V.G.I.," for "valley girl intelligentsia." Another was a memoir in which the guy got a crush on a barista and

one of the things that he liked was how cute her nails were, whereas his wife had apparently betrayed him by not having cute nails. And I thought the guy seemed shallow, and I also thought, I AM NOT GOING DOWN THAT WAY. Anyway, I did a reading once and a bookseller there and I got to talking. He said, "This local guy has an event tomorrow night," and it was THE FUCKING MANICURED BARISTA BOOK. And I held up my hand and I said, "This glitter is that guy's fault!" And the bookseller said, "Yeah, he's divorced now."

128. Nothing Annoys Me So Much
The stinginess of clocks. Surely they could lend us a few extra hours. There's never enough time to say all I want and hear all I want to and from you.

The feeling I had walking around with David in my life was that at last my soul had company. I gave thanks for him every day, especially when, having run a series of hour-devouring errands, he made me laugh. Having those emails to reread, especially on days when the world was too much with me—late and soon and at Tony's Auto Repair—made me feel rich. Every email felt like a fresh stack of library books.

At first he would ask if he was writing me too much. I asked him what part of Blanket Permission he didn't understand. He stopped asking and just sent me several messages a day, sometimes more than a dozen. He wrote: "I want to tell you so much. Why?! And when will it end, for chrissakes?!"

I kept asking: *Why did this happen? Why was I sent this person who felt like my destiny when I already had committed myself to someone for life? Was I double destined?* I couldn't tear myself away from him. There was just so much to get out.

He mailed me a little copy of Michel de Montaigne's *On Friendship* (1580): "In the friendship which I am talking about, souls are mingled and confounded in so universal a blending that they efface the seam which joins them together so that it cannot be found. If you press me to say why I loved him, I feel that it cannot be expressed except by replying: 'Because it was him: because it was me.'"

One night I was in a cab on the way back from a comedy show taping I'd gone to with a friend. They'd done a million takes and it had gone late. As the cab moved through nearly empty streets of Chinatown, I imagined David in the back seat of the cab with me. I turned my phone back on and saw that he had sent an uncharacteristically short email, though still in his typical formality:

"I love you, my dear, dear friend. I hope you share my pride in the great love we have created—a love greater than both of us, mysterious to both of us, and that you know as well as I do that this moment—tonight—that love is in a state of perfection."

My cheeks burned the way they did when I had to speak in front of the class as a shy child. There was no way I could unsee this email. Everything would change from this moment on. *Why was he doing this? Why did it need to be said?* There would be no coming back.

I put my phone down in my lap and looked out at the night. Between streetlamps, I caught my reflection in the window. I looked like I hadn't slept in days.

David had often talked about Nietzsche's concept of *amor fati*, how to love one's fate is to be content with what is. I knew that by saying what we had was perfect already he thought we didn't need to do anything about it; it could just exist. But he was wrong. He'd lived so much of his life in his own head that he didn't know what I did. Once those words were spoken, even if they were gussied up with Nietzsche, something did change, instantly and for-ever.

I felt the same way. Of course I did. But my mother and grandmother had taught me the value of holding on to a marriage. I knew this message about the depth of our love, now blazing on my phone—just waiting to be glimpsed by Paul—was one of the more obvious ways people got divorced. Our feelings were too strong.

"This has gotten too romantic," I replied. "Paul's permissiveness doesn't extend to this kind of declaration. We should tone it down."

Even as I protested, I felt something shift in me during that cab ride.

You know as well as I do.

I did know as well as he did, yes. But I knew something more than he did too—I knew that no matter how much philosophy we wrapped around our love, our fate would no longer sit still, letting itself be appreciated and accepted; now that it had been invoked, our fate was coming for us.

SEVEN

The Third Path

O ver Mexican food, a married friend of mine told me she'd had what she called a "crackle" with a man she'd met through work, that it was so *strange*. Nothing overtly sexual ever happened with the other man. She was strategic, avoided being alone with him, forced them to be family friends. He got married. They joke now about the early attraction. But she said it had been torment how she'd felt like there was no one to talk to about any of it. The detail she kept repeating was that at a conference cocktail party the man kept feeding her. She'd be talking to someone else and suddenly his hand was there, putting food directly into her mouth, saying, "You have to try this!"

She said that she was glad she'd gotten to experience desire for him and also managed to keep her marriage intact. Her husband had been concerned by the attraction, but during that time they'd had the best sex of their lives. That gave her hope that there was some way to handle such sparks in a nondestructive way. She told me about how another friend of hers was horrified that she still talked to the other man at all. This friend had been very flirtatious early in her life and went in the opposite direction once she married. Her rule for herself and her husband: "If we get attracted to someone we work with, we quit our jobs. If we get attracted to a neighbor, we move."

My dinner date said, sipping a margarita, that just by staying in touch with the other man she'd pushed things a little further than that all-or-nothing friend might have, but that she still hadn't let herself explore what more could have been possible. She'd always wondered if there were some other sort of relationship available with him.

Right! What was that perfect middle path between moving across town to save your marriage or "I live with my neighbor now"?

She didn't know. No one knew.

I once had a conversation with an agent about when a book I'd written should come out. Though the original plan was for September, my publisher was pushing for January. "They're the experts," I said. "They'd know."

"Oh, no one knows anything," my agent said, as if he were surprised I'd thought anyone did. "Almost nothing sells either, so you might as well do what you want."

When people said "I told you so" about open or open-ish marriages not working, I thought of other kinds of marriages—sexless, arranged, traditional, long distance. Do those always work out? What demographic has it completely figured out, start to finish, every time? When half of all marriages end, and plenty that last seem like perhaps they shouldn't? "Polyamory" had always sounded to me like a high school elective no one would choose to take. Why was I suddenly entertaining it?

The real danger, Veronica often said, was contorting ourselves to fit the status quo rather than paying attention to what we cared about: "What will do more damage than almost anything is to say, 'Here's the person I need to be in order to make this work, and so whatever it costs me, I'm going to be that way.'"

Paul started to notice, with mild concern, that all I talked about was David. But he also noticed that I was so incandescently happy that I wanted to have sex all the time. This, if I'd just stop seeming so moony, would have been a sign that I was finally on board with the adventuring he'd envisioned. He was all for the sexual charge; only the emotional part concerned him.

I told him not to worry about it, but keeping it under control had become another full-time job. I'd never lied to Paul, though I was glad he wasn't asking too many questions. I continued reading stacks of books on love each week in an effort to understand what was happening.

One was a 1923 German epistolary novel called *Zoo, or Letters Not About Love* by Viktor Shklovsky. In his preface, the author writes, "In an epistolary novel, the essential thing is motivation—precisely why should these people be writing to each other? The usual motivation is love and partings."

The man writing the letters is desperately in love with the woman, who doesn't have time for him, and so they have a prohibition against writing about love. What winds up happening is that the more they try not to talk about love, the more everything seems to become about love. The woman tells a long story about a wet nurse named Stesha and then asks, seeming shocked by her own disclosure: "Now what made me inflict Stesha on you?"

It doesn't matter whether you're saying you love and want each other; once you're inflicting Steshas, you don't have to.

One night while it rained outside, Paul and I sat talking after dinner, and he asked about David. He was wondering if he should be afraid that I'd run off with him. I said no. I was committed first and foremost to our marriage.

"This is a nourishing, interesting relationship that is not threatening or taking anything away from us," I said. "I feel closer to you than ever. If you feel uncomfortable at any point I will stop talking to him."

"Can I expect a lot of birthday presents to show your appreciation for how generous I'm being about David?"

"Of course," I said. I thought he might be joking but I wasn't sure, so I bought him a guitar.

Truly, I did feel grateful. "For the sin against the HOLY GHOST is INGRATITUDE," wrote seventeenth-century lunatic Christopher Smart, quoted by David in an email that he referred to as a "tractate." I vowed not to sin in that way. I still felt full of love for Paul—even more so for letting me have so much in my life outside of him.

Over Paul's birthday weekend, friends came over for every meal. I always had someone to talk to while I was making us pancakes, smoothies, sandwiches, lasagna. We played poker and Paul opened his presents. He loved the guitar.

Amid the celebrating, I noticed how secure Nate seemed. So many of my friends' parents and Nate's friends' parents had gotten divorced. I'd seen the toll it had taken on some of those whose parents had split up. They seemed unmoored for some period of time between a few months and the rest of their lives. If the gods of their childhood could make a promise in front of the whole world and then break it, who could be trusted?

Not to mention what it did to relationships between kids and their divorced parents. You couldn't predict it. One friend liked her philandering father's girlfriend more than her dutiful mother's new husband, and so she wound up living with her father. If I ever left Paul, dear God, what if Nate wound up staying with him whenever he was home from college? What if they celebrated holidays together, and for the rest of my life I only got brunch a few times a year at loud restaurants?

My son had become a kind and secure person. I didn't know how much having married parents was part of that, but I didn't want to find out. At dinner one night, as he took another taco off the stack I'd made, Nate told me that he sometimes wrote things and then when he read them back he was surprised by how good they were. He asked me if I'd had that feeling. I said I had. Once I wrote something about how my father hadn't cared that much about me, and I realized by writing it that it was true. And having said it out loud, I began to feel less sad about it.

"Aw, Mom!" he said, and came around the table and hugged me.

I thought, *You are welcome, world, for this remarkable person.* And I also thought: *Nothing is more important than preserving this child's sense of safety and home.*

"You and I raised our children to be people we wanted to know," Veronica liked to say. "And now we have children we love to be around."

My relationship with Nate and with almost everyone I knew was filtered through books in some way. I made my closest friends through reading one another's writing or by bonding over our love of other writers. Books are powerful—you have to give book banners that. You could be the best librarian on earth and not know what book will do what, when, to whom. Generations of people could read *The Sorrows of Young Werther* without incident. Are you going to ban it because a couple of them read it and then jumped off a bridge?

When he was little, I read to Nate more or less every single night. Thousands of hours. Once a week I brought home stacks of books from the library, as well as audiobooks for him to listen to on the CD player in his room. Valéry called lions "assimilated sheep." The way Nate spoke, even now as a teenager, was funny, warm, surprising—a ragù of P. G. Wodehouse, *Frog and Toad*, and World War II histories.

I worked hard to make our place comfortable for his friends and mine, and I liked having a home where people came when they needed help.

John, an old friend of the family who'd had a fire in his apartment, came over. I ordered us burgers, typed up his insurance inventory on my laptop, did his laundry, and gave him some replacement clothes he'd requested from Macy's. (My braving Macy's on a storewide-sale day was, I hoped he saw, a hall-of-fame display of friendship.) He told me that he'd been allowed to do one pass through his burned-up apartment before the building was demolished. The landlord shined a flashlight from one part of the room to another as he looked for things to salvage. "It might have been growing up Catholic," he said, "but as I left every room I whispered 'Goodbye, room.'" He mimed crossing himself.

John babysat his former girlfriend's kids. He worked at the food bank. After the fire, the community raised more than a hundred thousand dollars for him. He said he had the thought as he looked at all that money and at the hundreds of messages that came with it: *Maybe I'm . . . a good person?* After the burgers were eaten and the admin work and laundry done, I walked him to where he was staying. On each block he said hello to someone. At one point he stopped to pet a dog as he said to the owner, "He's gonna get bigger? How old is he? If you ever need a babysitter!"

Watching this person who'd just lost everything still smiling at strangers, I thought of my father. Even surrounded by good fortune and people who loved him, he'd moved through the world in a cloud of distraction and mild annoyance. Had he ever once offered a word of unselfconscious praise for a dog or a baby?

I didn't tell John about David, even though he was the only honest answer to the question, "What's new?" David and I were writing each other thousands of words a day. We read books and listened to music and talked about love and longing, fidelity and infidelity. We could not shut up; we always wanted more.

I encouraged him to watch mainstream movies he'd missed out on in his self-imposed austerity. He was a good student; I could tell because he started to make uncharacteristic references to pop culture. After I told him I was sorry for leaving a five-minute voicemail, he said, "Never apologize for that. Nothing you send is ever long enough. You could *Truman Show* that shit and I'd tune in."

We learned the word "limerence"—a term for involuntary obsession coined in the 1970s. I read definitions of the term as if I were receiving a diagnosis from a physician at a Swiss specialty clinic: "Limerence involves intrusive thinking.... A condition of sustained alertness... At peak crystallization, almost all waking thoughts revolve around the limerent object." The physical manifestations included shortness of breath and a sort of delirium. I hadn't inhaled fully in weeks. The air got caught somewhere.

How long did limerence last? According to one source, "From the moment of initiation until a feeling of neutrality is reached, is approximately three years. The extremes may be as brief as a few weeks or as long as several decades."

One morning at 7:54 a.m. I realized that I hadn't heard from David yet and I wondered if he would write that day, or if the fever had broken and the intensity had waned. *Maybe he won't write all weekend and that will be a sign that now we've reached neutrality.*

At 8:11, a tractate came through. It was about a twelfth-century book he had on his syllabus called *Spiritual Friendship*: "Friendship is that virtue, therefore, through which by a covenant of sweetest love our very spirits are united, and from many are made one."

He sent me photos of the title pages for his students' essays about creative forms of friendship. One was about "Boston marriages," where unmarried female friends lived together around the turn of the last century. Some of them were lesbian couples flying under the radar; others were friends who found a way to navigate the world together in a loving way. Another was about the *cicisbeo*, or *cavalier servente*, an acknowledged male mistress in eighteenth-century Italy.

"Did you turn your students into our unwitting research assistants?" I asked.

My real question, though, was how had what began as a simple college crush so quickly turned into a two-person cult?

Surely what was happening couldn't be bad or tawdry. It could be dumb, I supposed. It could be embarrassing or naïve. Certainly, it could fade away. And yet, apparently it could also last four months, four years, or four decades. All I knew was that honoring what we had seemed like a more valuable goal than trying to avoid looking stupid.

"I feel greedy to have all I have and want David too," I told Veronica.

"Is it greedy to crave human connection?" she said.

"Maybe," I said.

EIGHT

Full-Force Gale

Out of nowhere, Veronica's father, Bob, died. I went to his funeral by the ocean, where he'd retired after a lifetime of meaningful public service and lovingly raising three daughters my age. At the memorial, I watched one person after another take the stage and talk about what he'd done for them.

One said, "I'm another of the lost boys the girls brought home because life was rough at my place. Bob took me out and talked to me about books. He said, 'All philosophy agrees on the way to live a good life: Be born to a rich and noble family. You screwed that up, so we need to figure out something else for you.'" Then he did. So many people in that crowd had good lives, happy kids running around, because of what that man did for them.

Throughout the service I sat in the row behind Veronica and occasionally put my hand on her shoulder. I was glad she couldn't see me cry; the tears were more for myself than for her anyway. Bob and my father had both been bohemians and both had daughters. My father, so different from Veronica's, had cancer, and it wasn't clear how many months he had left. When the time came for his funeral, I could not imagine anyone saying that when it came to love he'd given more than he got.

Love filled the room at Bob's service, and love welled up in my heart every time I heard from David. Plutarch said that "lovers themselves believe, and would have all others think, that the object of their passion is pleasing and excellent." I kept wanting to turn to the person next to me and brag like the proudest parent at the school recital: "That's my kid up there!" Only in David's case it would be: "That's my *whatever he is* sharing another pearl of wisdom! Isn't he smart? And handsome too? Here's a picture! Here's another picture! Here's—where are you going?"

Emerson pointed to an intimacy beyond romantic love. Learning that lesson, David and I could avoid getting caught up in anything physical, temporal, or earthly. Our love could grow and spread outward into the world. We could see that not as a sacrifice but as a gift.

At the funeral reception, one of Veronica's aunts monologued to me about her garden for twenty minutes, and
my attention never flagged. A four-year-old clung to me
like we were on a sinking ship, and I wound up cleaning
an entire globe's worth of fake *Frozen*-themed snow off
her buffet plate. In my state of limerence I'd somehow
passed mindfulness and intentionality and entered a new
state of total presence.

Full presence was my mantra. Veronica had always said
that if you're truly focused, "very, very present," no matter how difficult a situation is, you can download Apache
helicopter instructions to your brain like they do in *The
Matrix*. And that's what I was trying to do every second.
I made meals each day for my family. The house was
well kept. I was at inbox zero.

"I've noticed you don't check your phone anymore
when we're together," Veronica said. "Not that it really
bothered me, but it's nicer now." In my joy at beholding
the world so closely and carefully I believed that nothing
could go wrong.

The night of the funeral Veronica came to my hotel
for dinner and decided to stay for a slumber party, and
so briefly escape her aunts and cousins with their land-
scaping stories and Dollar Store toys. As we sat on the
balcony of my—now our—room and looked out at the

ocean, I read her one of David's emails. She'd been following along as we'd grown close, but she'd never heard
his writing voice before, and she looked surprised.

"Is he a character in a Russian novel?" she said. "Why
does he talk like that?"

I explained to her that after initially finding his messages bewildering I began to adjust to their language
and tempo. As I did, I found that each one made me
think of a thousand things to say. I was writing back
from some until then untouched part of my mind and
heart. My replies to him struck me as some of the best
writing I'd ever done. I loved who I was when I was talking to him.

I told her about the British writer Charles Williams,
who wrote a hundred years ago about moments when "a
hand lighting a cigarette is the explanation of everything; a foot stepping from the train is the rock of all
existence." Williams, one of the Inklings with J. R. R.
Tolkien and C. S. Lewis, described a form of mystical
vision in which we saw the person we loved "as he or she
was seen through the eyes of God." With David, that was
how I saw myself too.

"You've certainly caught feelings, haven't you?" she said.

She liked Paul. I liked him too, I reassured her. I had
this all under control. David and I had never even kissed,

even though Paul had said I should kiss people. We were so saturated by books and songs and poems that I felt that it was more a research project than an affair. I imagined saying to her, "Affair? No! We are just ascending a ladder to pure language!" She let it drop, and I was glad. Then I excused myself to check my email. I hoped I'd have a long message from David, and I did.

I'd sent him a photo of fog over the water along with the W. H. Auden poem, one of the last he ever wrote, "Thank You, Fog." His gratitude came from the joy of spending time with friends at a country house so shrouded in fog that there was no reason to leave their cozy company.

David had replied with this from Rabindranath Tagore, the Bengali poet: "The feeling which I had was like that which a man, groping through a fog without knowing his destination, might feel when he suddenly discovers that he stands before his own house."

My own house. Something about that phrase seemed to encapsulate how I felt about David. He was my *house.* We still hadn't discussed attraction, only shock at having found in each other a kind of twin. The truth was, Paul had sanctioned sexy flings, not full-blown romantic entanglements. And so for David and me to be alone together, much less to kiss, seemed unwise. We lived in different cities. People in our situation got tractates or benders, not both, and we were choosing the former.

If anything, what we were having was an intellectual affair, even if David did keep using phrases like "a covenant to fulfill." I didn't know what that meant, but I believed that if loving someone but not taking that feeling to its logical conclusion was an Olympic sport, I was at the mall rink every day working on my triple axel.

I didn't know how David was making time to write so much to me. I wondered if he was neglecting his students. I began to worry that I was becoming a member of the B-52's "Deadbeat Club," the equivalent of a stoner roommate always trying to get him to stay home and play video games. I asked if I should leave him alone more.

"I'm here for all of it," he said, "especially the jangling shiny objects that are emitting sparks of holy light."

Psychologist Adam Phillips called lovers "frantic epistemologists," "readers of signs and wonders." And I saw signs for us everywhere. After Veronica fell asleep, I stayed up wondering if I was spending too much time talking to David. I flipped on TCM. A 1949 movie called *Holiday Affair* was just coming on. Two men pursue a war widow played by twenty-two-year-old Janet Leigh. Carl, the one who's not Robert Mitchum, gives her up because she loves Robert Mitchum best. When she says she's sorry to have wasted so much of his time, Carl says, "No time is wasted that makes two people friends." I took that as reassurance that whatever was happening, it was something good.

At a diner breakfast with Veronica the next morning I was making faces at a baby in the booth behind us when the mother handed me the baby to hold.

"Why do people always want to hand you their babies?" Veronica said. "No one ever hands me babies."

"Do you want them to?" I said.

"Not really," she said.

"See? That's why."

Turning to the mother I said, "She's adorable, and seems very smart. What's her name?"

"Cherish," her mother said.

"Cherish!" I said, almost flinging the baby back at her mother so I could text David, who'd just used that word in his email the night before.

Everything that happened became valuable to the degree it was worth telling him.

"Why am I telling you this?" he often asked after a story about his day. "Because I want to tell you everything."

NINE

Abundance

I don't know if I should be jealous, because I don't really know what the hell this is," Paul said of my relationship with David as he made dinner and I worked at the kitchen table. "You're not kissing him even though you have permission. It's not purely emotional, sexual, intellectual, or a friendship. It's got some of all of these, but it feels like something new. Mostly I'm just impressed."

Family life was better than ever. I played Uno with Nate. (New rule: when you won you had to yell, "Uno Out!") I took him shopping for jeans, compulsively cleaned the house, set out bright flowers, grilled fish for dinner. At night, when Paul was out with friends, I wrote back and forth with David.

I'd look at an inbox of thirty-six new emails, many

from famous people, and the only message I'd care about was the one from David telling me whether or not he liked the new cover of the Replacements' "Skyway" on our shared playlist. I had a tall stack of manuscripts on my desk to edit and blurb but the only thing I wanted to read was a sexy Octavio Paz poem David had mentioned in passing.

Every second of every day felt more worthwhile now that he was in my life. And I looked forward to going to bed because as soon as I turned the light out and closed my eyes, there he was. As in Jonathan Richman's song "Astral Plane," if I couldn't see him in real life, I'd see him in my dreams.

Paul had chosen to be philosophical and capacious about all of it. "Our love is abundant," he said. "Abundance means we can spare it. There is no need to hoard love. There's *plenty*. Creation is an abundance of love. We should be giving it away in little ways all day and in big ways all our lives." I thought about how love and money both so often go to people who already have them. It's hardest to acquire money when you're broke and to find love when you're lonely.

Paul saw his occasional flickers of jealousy as a welcome spiritual challenge, especially because my desire to keep him on board made me more forgiving of things

about which I'd formerly been critical. Paul knew everything that was happening. I figured that because we were
still attracted to each other we were doing well as a couple. He was happy to see me happy.

"I don't want it to be that I'm the wall and you're Pyr-
amus and Thisbe," he said. "Or that I'm the blood feud
and you're Romeo and Juliet."

He felt that my friendship with David was making his
life better too. We felt proud of ourselves for making
space for this kind of life-giving connection. He began to
talk about how he'd like to find a close friendship like
that too. I would have been a hypocrite to say no, though
I did feel strange about the notion of his pursuing other
people for this sort of deep connection. But he was being
so considerate about David; how could I begrudge him
anything?

He offered an analogy to what he saw as our willing-
ness to create space for something that might make others uncomfortable. He had a friend who worked as a
technical director for theaters. Paul said tech people often started with a list of rules: No glitter, no liquids, no
hanging anything from the ceiling. But this guy started
all conversations with a simple question: "What do you
want to do?" He'd work with you to try to figure out how
to make it work, how to let you do the show you wanted

to do. *Maybe glitter was fine if there were a tarp. Maybe if we rigged pulleys we could . . .*

That seemed like a strategy for a lasting marriage, and for a richer life than past generations of women were able to have. You could come at commitment from a place not of rules but of *Tell me what you want. Let's see if we can figure out how you can have it.* That doesn't mean infinite permission. The technical director would have to say, often, "That's not possible." But there was a reason why. And he always had a plan B, something that was sometimes even better than the original proposal.

So that's what Paul and I were doing, I decided: a new and better kind of fidelity, a fidelity to each other and to ourselves. That didn't mean there was never static. As Paul, Nate, and I pulled into our auto repair shop for an oil change, Paul pointed to one of the techs and asked, "Is that your boyfriend?" He knew someone there always went out of his way to be extra helpful when I brought in the car.

"No, that's Evan. He's also lovely. But my boyfriend here is Kris."

Nate, from the back seat, said, "I thought Tom Hanks was your boyfriend."

"Your mother has a lot of boyfriends," Paul said.

I heard an edge in his voice.

TEN

Permission

There used to be a video store near our home staffed by a young couple. They showed movies in the back room for kids every weekend—*Paper Moon* almost caused a riot because of the little girl smoking—and the adults could sit in the front room drinking Bloody Marys and eating popcorn. It was about as great a gift to parents of young children as has ever existed on this earth.

Nate never missed a film. His laminated punch card filled up fast. He had a bronze one, then silver, then gold . . . then they didn't know what to do because no one else had seen that many movies. They asked him what color he wanted. And so he came to possess the only ruby video card in existence.

David would have had the only ruby card if I'd given out punch cards, though I didn't know what exactly ours would signify. The relationship seemed to be dictating its own terms. One day, after confessing that he'd seen every bit of footage of me online, he said, "Frankly, if it weren't so wholesome and mutual, it's the kind of thing that might be scary." He named his favorite clip.

"My dress was too tight," I said.

"Was it? I didn't notice," he said, in a way that made it clear he certainly had noticed.

As I'd grown more philosophical, he had apparently become less monk-like.

I thought of a line I'd heard about problems just being questions asked in the wrong way. We would only need to find the right way to ask what we were to each other, the best databases and search terms, and everything could be figured out in no time! We had library cards and mo-tivation. I had the honor-student's confidence that with enough hard work there was nothing that could not be understood.

We made a list:

What the fuck is this?

What do we owe each other? What do we owe ourselves?

What do we want from each other? What do we want from our-selves?

We who leave a tradition must have something better in mind, right? What?

Who are we when we're at our best?

We kept searching one library and bookstore after another for clues to what we were feeling and what to do about it. We were broadcasters on election night in the early days of television, ties loosened, jackets off, running electoral-vote scenarios on a chalkboard even after the viewers at home had gone to bed.

Here's one of the things we found, from Sheila Heti:

"All this seemed to be happening of its own accord, this laying down of a bridge on which things between them could pass; not necessarily sexual things, or even intimate things, but things as yet unknown."

Here's another, from a passage in a book about the Chinese court concept of an "intimate friend": "The most deeply felt affinities between people were likened to 'soundless music' . . . True friends consider themselves stupendously lucky to have encountered one another . . . intimate friendship hardly qualifies as completely 'voluntary' in the modern sense."

That was right! Nothing about what we were experiencing felt voluntary! We made each other better too. Without my levity, he could be opaque. Without his gravity, I could become distracted from what was truly important. Of Fred Astaire and Ginger Rogers it was said, "He gave her class, and she gave him sex appeal." I turned him on to 1980s movies and he introduced me to Annie Dillard. We joked that we were John and Yoko, and he was Yoko. I'd be the one saying, "Let's write a song called 'Help!'" And he'd say, "Yes! Or how about a *Tsurezuregusa*?"

I tried to convince myself of the plausibility that I'd never spend time around David and that I would not suffer from the lack of it, but I also began fantasizing about holding his hand. If he were a record it would have been all scratched up. If he were an item of clothing he would have been threadbare.

Even as I worked very hard to make him and whatever he and I had into a research project and a symbol of safe expansion, I did begin to suspect that we'd become the romantic equivalent of two very drunk people convincing each other that they are excellent drivers. We were both eager to throw each other the car keys, stumble down the driveway, hit the road.

I thought back to the closest thing I'd ever had to this feeling before. It was twenty years earlier, when Paul and I were still boyfriend-girlfriend, not yet engaged. I'd gotten a crush on a friend—in truth, it was far beyond a crush. I broke it off as if it had been nothing. I talked about it as if it had been nothing. But it was definitely *something*.

I made the break for what I thought were good reasons. I bought into the idea that "cheating" was "bad," that to be "faithful" to your partner was "good." But was it good to have two loves in your hand and to fling one away? I suffered. He suffered. I broke both our hearts. I thought that was the price we had to pay for falling in love when I already had a boyfriend, when I was "taken."

In talking to David I began to realize that I'd committed a sin against that man, but even more so against myself, by giving him up the way I had. David felt sorry for me. He said, "Most sins inflict their punishment on the sinner above all. Heaven and hell are contained in the deeds themselves—I think Blake said that."

At the time, ending it made me feel virtuous. I'd seen *Brief Encounter*! I'd seen *Lonesome Dove*! I knew what was supposed to happen! You were supposed to choose! And so I chose. And how could I regret the choice when I'd stayed with the man I chose for so long and we'd had a family? Without that choice who knows if I'd have had children at all, much less my perfect son. Once I'd sacrificed another love for Paul, I knew that whatever happened I would stay with him and so justify that choice. If

I'd refused my friend for a less-than-eternal love that would have been a heresy. But if I'd left him for the man I'd spend the rest of my life with, then it was clearly the right thing to do.

Still, ever since I'd felt remorse without knowing quite what I should have done differently. Many times I'd be walking through town, and I'd imagine that any second I might see that other man. I wondered if he'd stop to talk or blow past me. I wondered if he'd forgive me if I said I was sorry. I wondered if he should. What else could I have done? In the past I'd asked that question rhetorically. Now I was asking it in all seriousness: *For real, what else could I have done?*

Whatever it was, could I do that now? Was this the chance to do it right? A chance for redemption? To have two loves and not reject one just to maintain some preconceived idea of what relationships were supposed to look like?

Fidelity to yourself and to other people, how to love well, and faith in the goodness of the world—those were the themes of what I was reading. What did love dare us to do? If David was making me feel more like myself, if I was fully present as a wife, mother, and friend—and I'd never been so present in my life, that was a fact—where was the danger? No, really, where was it?

One day as I sat at my desk wondering what it would be like to feel David holding me, I heard a neighbor's cat in heat. For days the yowling was relentless. So many people said something that the neighbors put a sign on their window that said: PLEASE LEAVE THE HORNY CAT ALONE.

At our last staff meeting David and I had talked about whether we could or should see each other in person. We decided it was probably better not to. I believed that with my heart and I was resolved. The neighbor's cat cried from another, far less evolved, universe.

David and I didn't want to complicate things. We didn't want to be common. So we were not going to be like the cat. We were going to be sober and mature. We worked on the problem of what to do about safely containing our love like it was our job.

Day after day, he sent me photos of pages he was reading, looking for an answer. In such photos, my eye went to his thumb holding down the page before I saw the words. I saw worlds in the wrinkles at his knuckles, the tension with which he held the books. The truth was I just wanted to see him *so bad*. It was all I could think about. Every night, the cat's howls echoed down the street. I really wished that cat would shut the fuck up.

ELEVEN

Heloise and Abelard

For decades, I filled a journal once or twice a year. From the time I started talking to David, I finished a whole composition notebook each week. Before, I read a book a month; now I skimmed at least two a day. David compiled the first six weeks of our correspondence into a single document; he reported that it was 182,000 words long. No matter how many emails and texts, there was always more to say. I wondered what might feel like enough.

After that first Zoom, we began to meet that way once a week, sometimes for two hours at a time. We texted. We started a shared Google doc. If we'd had fax machines or a telephone made of tin cans and string, I think we would have used those too. And my fantasies evolved.

Now I was daydreaming of kissing his neck, lying in a bed with him, touching his face . . .

I knew I'd fallen in love with Paul, but that had been so long ago. I wondered if maybe I'd forgotten how it felt, the way people forget the pain of childbirth (though I had not forgotten that), but I didn't remember it being so all-consuming. I needed to stay married though. I'd made a promise, and I intended to keep it. My mother did not raise me not to keep promises. If she'd managed to stay with her husband, surely I could stick it out with mine.

I'd just have to make some rules for myself and live by them. And so I decided to keep a boundary, one that would let us continue to talk as much as we liked: we'd simply never be alone in a room together. There was only so much damage we could do from afar. Our patron saints would be Heloise and Abelard corresponding from their respective religious orders.

Their twelfth-century letters were sexy, but only in reminiscing about their former connection, back when he'd been her tutor, before her family had gotten him castrated. He wrote: "We were united, first under one roof, then in heart; and so with our lessons as a pretext we abandoned ourselves entirely to love. Her studies allowed us to withdraw in private, as love desired, and then with our books open before us, more words of love than of our reading passed between us, and more kissing than teaching."

We could imagine a kiss but enjoy our distance, which would make room for a powerful lifelong friendship. The way we'd keep things perfect would be to keep them distant, as they had been for Heloise and Abelard even after she wrote, "If the name of wife appears more sacred and more valid, sweeter to me is ever the word friend, or, if you be not ashamed, concubine or whore."

"Now seems a moment to live deliberately," David said. "And while we've never wanted to outsmart love—only embody it fully—if we are going to make ambitious demands of our love, we'd better know what we are demanding."

We were committed to sacrifice, even though the attraction was growing like a magic beanstalk. My desire was everything I'd been led to believe was possible when in my adolescence I'd encountered the erotic one-two punch of *Jane Eyre* and the *Family Ties* episode where Michael J. Fox gets together with Tracy Pollan.

More and more, I felt that David and I weren't in control of how we felt. I wanted to kiss him more than I'd ever wanted anything. I wanted more, too, but that was as far as I'd let myself go even in my fantasy life. I'd always had excellent willpower. But not anymore. I wouldn't have trusted myself in a hotel room with him, nor in an elevator, nor even seated next to him in a dark restaurant. . . . I could have gone full *Green Eggs and Ham* describing my desire and what a movable feast it was. But I believed we could turn it into something productive rather than destructive. What we could do with that feeling if, as sober, responsible adults, we could contain it! We could power a city!

"Your marriage is important to you and so it's important to me," David said. "Of course if you were free things might be different. But this is our spiritual challenge, and we are surely learning from it."

We had heat-reduction strategies beyond emulating Heloise and Abelard postcastration. We took days off from writing to each other. Well, we tried to take days off and wound up taking half days off, but it was something. He kept a list during those interludes of all the times he'd wanted to be in touch. The numbers were spaced out by a few minutes. I felt his absence like a phantom limb.

Early in the pandemic shutdowns, there was talk about "the hammer and the dance," where you'd relax the rules gradually, dancingly, and then when things got rough you'd bring the hammer down, and then after a while you'd dance back out again. That was more or less what we were doing. We started texting until we realized that the flirtation had spun out of control, so we stopped, judging the moonlight too strong for us. Then we grew frustrated at having to email photos of book pages and resumed texting all day.

As best I could, I distracted myself with work, including teaching and mentoring, writing essays, and cowriting a television pilot.

"We should write a book together," David said one day during a staff meeting.

"What would it be about?"

"Us? It could be called *This (Whatever It Is)*."

Whatever it was called, I began to believe that it would be the best book I'd ever write or read. In any case, what was I going to do, walk away from the question? Besides, writing a book about our mysterious connection might give us some critical distance, sublimate our longing into something potentially useful.

We agreed that this would let us have a purely epistolary affair, the perfect, safe affair—Abelard and Heloise 2.0. We didn't have to give each other up to be good. We compiled a short commonplace-book's worth of aphorisms about how perfection is overrated.

He quoted Randall Jarrell: "A good poet is someone who manages, in a lifetime of standing out in thunderstorms, to be struck by lightning five or six times; a dozen or two dozen times and he is great."

I replied with the Ted Williams line "Baseball is the only field of endeavor where a man can succeed three times out of ten and be considered a good performer."

Yes, we would canalize our feelings into work. I wrote up a proposal:

"*This (Whatever It Is)* is an epistolary memoir. A casual exchange between two people led to a torrent of long emails back and forth all day, every day, about what we were doing and reading and thinking. We read the same books, listened to the same music, and our letters kept circling around the question of what to do with each other that wasn't the usual thing people do in such situations, which is either to stop speaking or have a disastrous affair. We rallied every relevant resource like we were living in *The Arabian Nights*, only we were both Scheherazade.

"Together we worked tirelessly to answer questions like: What do you do with overwhelming relationships that don't quite fit into your life? Can you have intimacy without consummation? Can you make room in your daily life for spiritual love? Our struggle to find a vocabulary to discuss our liminal relationship, to be close without transgression, to be true friends to each other—these questions consumed us. Ultimately, we contained the attraction that had drawn us together and realized that these conversations might serve others encountering what Emerson called 'a wandering spark,' those longing to love and be loved without causing others harm."

I told Paul about this book plan, expecting that he'd be relieved. Now we had something to call David: my collaborator. Collaborators talked all the time, didn't they? We had to talk a lot, *for the book.*

Paul looked skeptical. He said he had two rules if we wrote a book:

"One: I will not throw a book party where you and David sit on stools at the front of the room mooning over each other. Two: The book must not be called *The Greatest Love of All: How an Inconvenient Love Changed My Life.* If it is, I will throw a car."

"I never thought of that title but it's not bad," I said. "Because that song 'The Greatest Love of All' is about loving yourself. Whitney Houston is singing about learning to love what's inside of you, not someone else. And I think that's the point of whatever we're working on. It's not a romance, but rather through talking to each other we're learning more about who we're meant to be in the world."

"I will *throw a car,*" Paul said.

TWELVE

Game Plans

Valéry wrote, "Hope sees a chink in the armor of the scheme of things." And so David and I continued on our treasure hunt through the history of world literature for inspiration. We decided that as long as we were being considerate and responsible toward everyone else in our lives—particularly my family and his students—we could keep up what we were doing, with the golden rule: "If it increases love, it's virtuous. If it decreases love, it's vicious."

Catching Veronica up one day as we sat in the park I concluded my short lecture with, "So you see, we just have to choose, at every turn, to make the more loving choice!"

She made a face.

"What?" I said. "How can you find fault with making loving choices?"

"Did you crib this foundational rule from *Highlights* magazine?" she said, shaking her head. "Because this sounds a lot like that cartoon, *Goofus and Gallant*: 'Gallant holds the door for the older lady; Goofus lets it slam in her face.' 'Gallant pets the dog; Goofus kicks it.'"

"Outside of pediatricians' waiting rooms and eight-year-olds' brains, choices are much more complicated than that. You can ignore the dog, write a poem about the dog, train the dog to talk. Everything you're calling 'good' can backfire. The 'bad' can turn out to be the best thing for everyone. Adults deal in moral ambiguity. Never hurting people or getting hurt is impossible if you're living an honest life."

"I'm not living an honest life?" I asked indignantly. "I'm a goddamned paragon of my community!"

"Yes, the community loves sacrifice, and you've done that well. But no, it's not honest. Deep down, I think you want more and that you're angry. And that you're right to be."

I wrote down the conversation so I could bring it to David, yet another offering, just as he was taking notes on everything he heard for me. Both of us were lighting candles every day on our shared altar.

In Robert Musil's *The Man Without Qualities*, a great scientist is asked how he manages to come up with so much that is new. His reply: "Because I never stop thinking about it."

David and I were like that. And surely this attention would be rewarded with a breakthrough.

Only it was getting harder and harder to be apart. I wanted to hold him. I didn't know when I'd ever wanted anything more, or when I'd been more conflicted about what that would mean. I imagined us inside a Choose Your Own Adventure where at the end of a scene you are presented with a choice: "Do you go inside the cave? Turn to page 65," or "Do you take the potion? Turn to page 7."

Here, as I saw it, were the different Choose Your Own Adventure plots we could follow as two people kept apart by circumstance. *Turn to . . .*

page 51: Stoic renunciation (*Brief Encounter, Age of Innocence*—practical, wistful)

page 19: Run off together; caught and punished (Hollywood—messy, potentially "Wave of Mutilation"–style destructive)

page 92: Socially approved but circumscribed long-term physical and/or emotional and/or intellectual affair (the French?—enlivening, dangerous) *page 33*: Double suicide (Shakespeare/*Dateline*—tragic, gruesome)

page 14: Contained sublimation (only example might be Viktor Shklovsky's *Zoo*???—cool, tricky!)

"Obviously, double suicide is off the table," I wrote to David. "Sublimation seems like our stated and excellent goal. I fear renunciation as an inevitable necessity of failing to successfully pull off the others. I also fear the statistical likelihood of punishment when sending too many messages of adoration through hackable channels (which is all of them). Actually, now that I'm looking at it, I guess my lurking worst-case scenario has been that we fail at sublimation (and I'd know it was definitely my fault because you are an ascetic by nature, but I am occasionally persuasive), so then we wind up unable to control this, at which point the only option left would be renunciation. But most of the time I believe we can totally pull off page 14!"

What would have happened if he'd never done what he did next? Would page 14 have been possible? I'm not sure, but here is what he did:

"I think we should see each other in person, even if it's only once. I have to go to California in a couple of months to present a paper at a religion symposium. I want you to join me."

Nabokov wrote that the wise reader reads the book of

genius not with his mind or heart but with his spine. That email of his I read with my spine.

"I want to, of course," I said. "I'll think about it. In the meantime, you can change your mind if you want."

"I won't change my mind," he said.

For a new perspective, I saw an old friend for coffee. With her I was able to talk about the most important things with no restraint even if we went a year without seeing each other. Our three-hour talks were both exhaustive and nourishing. I knew she'd help me decide what to do with David.

"Wow!" she said after hearing about him. "He's your soulmate collaborator! That's the most important thing! All the rest is in service of that! Martin Buber in *I and Thou* said, 'All actual life is encounter,' and 'The world is not comprehensible, but it is embraceable.' Is it possible that in some way your destiny is connected to this other person, and you're just trying to figure out in what way?" She asked when I would see him. I told her about California.

"Does that sound sordid?" I asked.

She shook her head.

"You have to ask: *If this was my last year alive, how would I want to spend it? If I had thirty years?* If you're saying 'Things are good enough—why should I blow them up?' The answer is because 'good enough' should not be the goal," she said. "We didn't work this hard"—by "we" I sensed she meant women—"to be *fine*."

For so long I'd been fine. Truly fine. I'd wanted nothing but to enjoy the fruits of my labor—marriage, career, friends, community. When I felt blue I'd double down on doing good out in the world; I found it usually cheered me up. I held babies, got ice cream for my parents, told my kid I was proud of him. I felt like if I died I could feel at peace with how I'd chosen to live my life. And yet, whatever I did now, someone was sure to get hurt eventually.

"You're lit up," she said, as if she were a doctor giving me the opposite of a fatal prognosis. "You're glowing. As a creative person this is where you have to live. And it's all here, right?" she said, and she ran her right hand gently along her left forearm. "The creative, the spiritual, it's in our bodies. Why wouldn't touching be a part of it too?"

THIRTEEN

A Thimble or a Vase

At first, my father's diagnosis had made him gentler and more thoughtful. Then his former self returned with a vengeance. He repeatedly delivered the same proclamations, anticipating praise or at least tacit agreement. One old standard was about how when someone got a tattoo, something he had never done, that person was saying "I'll always feel *just like this!*"

Only one day as he concluded his tattoos-are-stupid maxim, that line I'd listened to in silence a thousand times, I piped up, "No! That's not what they're saying! They're saying, 'I never want to forget this!' Tattoos are a remnant of someone you used to love or someplace you went or some time when you were immature, maybe.

But why do you have to mock people for caring about things?"

Why was I not able to let it slide? I had no tattoos. I had no investment in this argument. Why did I choose that moment to raise an objection? Had David's sincerity converted me? It had always been rare that I argued. I'd never hit anyone with my fists or with my car. Unlike my father, I was a slow, patient driver, happy to zip the zipper when merging, to defer to others if there were any question about whose turn it was. I was not the type of person to yell at a dying man about the hypothetical meaning of tattoos. But with my father I'd become weirdly edgy.

He'd become that way with me too. He said that my disappointment in his parenting when I was a child was really on me, that I should have worked harder to connect with him. He told me that his friends didn't like me. They thought I gave him too hard a time, and so they wanted to avoid my company. He shrugged and turned his hands upward as if their defense of him was something beyond his control. He smirked.

"Why would you tell me any of that unless you wanted to hurt me?" I said and started crying. "Even if they hate me like you say they do, why would you enjoy making sure I knew it? How could you be so unloving?"

"I don't have the capacity to love," he said, no longer

smiling, though not particularly moved by my tears. "I don't feel *loved* either. It's like my heart is a thimble." He held his fingers near his heart. "However much love comes in it just fills up that thimble and the rest goes on the floor. I don't take in any more. And that's about how much I have to give too."

"That's depressing," I said.

He shrugged.

"And it's a cop-out!"

I told him about the bell hooks book that David and I had just read, how she talked about love as something you do, not something you feel. She said that love was a verb, and that love was as important as work. I thought of a quote by Meister Eckhart, who compared love to a vessel that grows as it's filled and so can't ever be full. I pictured a vase swelling and swelling, growing to the size of a house.

I described to my father ways my mother and I showed him love and suggested he could just copy those. For example, I made sure that whenever he came over, the root beer he liked was in the fridge. Why didn't he just help my mother with dinners? When he was in town buying cigarettes, he could pick up a pizza so for one night a week she didn't have to cook? When a kid rattles on for a long time about his Pokémon cards, you didn't have to deliver some devastatingly witty put-down. You could just say, "Wow, that seems like a lot of hit points." How hard is that?

He asked me for the name of the books I mentioned. I told him. He didn't write them down.

FOURTEEN

A Room Without a Door

When I mentioned the California trip possibility one night as we were getting ready for bed, Paul took in a sharp inhale of breath. He seemed to be thinking hard as he brushed his teeth. When he was done, he said, "On one hand, I find this scenario extremely hot. On the other, the emotional intensity freaks me out. I can think of another question to add to your research project: In writing so much about not having a run-of-the-mill affair are you doing exactly that? Are you so smart you're stupid?"

In her 1996 song "Shameless," Ani DiFranco sings about how she and this person who is married find themselves together in a room without a door. She predicts that other people are coming and will find them, and when they do they'll be mad. They'll want to know how they got into the doorless room—and more importantly, what their plan is for getting out. We had reached the chorus of that song.

"No one is driving this train," Paul said, "not you, not him. We have to just see where it ends up. I'm the planet you live on, to quote that song you like. Other men have been like shooting stars, but this guy is fully another planet. I hope you don't leave me for him. You really shouldn't, by the way! I'm cool! He's a nerd! He's the kind of guy you marry; I'm the kind you have an affair with. The way you two write to each other gives me pause more than you sleeping with him. I don't think any of this ends without pain and tears. It might work out, but it won't be simple.

"You've read so much"—Paul said, casting an arm out in the direction of my bookshelf, crowded with books about limerence and friendship—"but even you can't outsmart love. You're going to the library to try to make sense of something you're unable, or unwilling, to face in real life: you want each other. And that part I'm into, but when energy has no boundaries it can become chaotic. You really should put down the transcendentalists and read *Polysecure*."

"If anyone can find a way to love each other without breaking containers, we can!" I said. "We've worked so hard to increase and not decrease love! This is our project—facing up to the reality that these things are usually doomed but finding our way to a happy ending!"

"If you see him in person, you have no idea what will be unlocked," Paul said. "But I'm not going to be the one to stop you."

If I was paying attention to what I cared about, everything was clear. I wanted to be the person I was with David. I felt more fully myself. I felt connected to something I couldn't explain, something life-giving. Our friendship felt—and everything I said now sounded insane even to me—holy.

For all his initial promotion of polyamory, Paul had begun to add caveats. He liked the idea of me as a sexual being in the world. He was glad that I was finally seeing things his way. And yet, he was afraid of what might happen when I went to California.

He wanted it made clear that this time with David would be a holiday, not my real life. He said that all societies had found ways to siphon off emotions that didn't fit inside of approved social institutions like marriage: "Bacchanals, Fat Tuesday, jubilee years, Carnival . . . There are ways to ritualistically contain these things. We just need to respect the container. You can go see

him, but it would be outside the everyday. You're creating a hypercircumscribed magical space. A trip would
be your Shrove Tuesday, not open-ended. Or you could
just not go. Why try to see him?"

The real answer was because if I didn't hold him in
my arms immediately I thought I would implode. And I
believed that I could handle it. I was delirious, but I wasn't
dumb. I knew that at some point something might shift,
that I'd want to be with him instead of Paul. But with
everyone working hard to keep that from happening, I
had faith that the threat was remote. I believed that I
was mature enough to remain composed. Yes, if we were
all in our twenties I might run after him, but we were *old*.
We knew that just because you *felt* something didn't mean
you had to *do* anything about it. And as far as I was concerned, divorce was off the table.

When a decade earlier a friend of mine got divorced,
women he dated sent him sexy pictures. He'd sometimes
show them to me on his phone while our kids were
nearby doing arts and crafts and eating buttered pasta.
One Halloween a woman he'd broken up with appeared
at his door heartbroken, weeping, cat makeup running
down her face. I've thought often of that crying cat. That's
the kind of embarrassing scene that, as I had come to
understand, came standard issue with divorce. I liked to

believe that I'd be dignified even in the face of such loss, but we never know what we're capable of, not really.

"You wouldn't have to worry about that," David said when I told him the crying cat story, as I told him every story. "If you ever got divorced, Penelope, you'd have suitors lined up for blocks." I looked it up: in *The Odyssey*, when Odysseus is away Penelope has 108 suitors—52 from Dulichium, 24 from Same, 20 from Zacynthus, and 12 from Ithaca. "Again: I share your goal of protecting your marriage. Of course, if you ever left it, I'd be asking different questions."

I shook off that sort of talk. We could do better. We would do better.

FIFTEEN

The PowerPoint Presentation

You and David better not be doing that!" Paul said. We were watching TV when two of the show's characters who'd been on an amusement-park date started making out and expressing their feelings for each other.

"Playing mini golf?" I said, though I knew what he meant.

He'd begun to feel left out and overwhelmed. I wanted to reassure him, and I tried. I also did not know what was going to happen once I saw David. If we were strategic about it would we burn off the desire? Or would it grow stronger? Would being together in person ramp up the erotic or tamp it down?

Paul: "What's the *plan* exactly? I don't want you sleeping in a bed with someone else. That's more intimate than sex. If you have sex with someone else, that turns me on. If you're cuddling with them, I want to start breaking dishes."

"If I'm going on this trip, I'll ask that you not make me travel with lists of approved and unapproved line items. I've slept in the same bed with other people plenty of times," I said. "Remember when Veronica and I shared a bed the night of her dad's funeral?"

He rolled his eyes. "You know that is very different."

"You were the one who wanted me to be with other men in the first place," I said. "What did you think it would be like?"

Asking Paul for shore leave to go see David with no rules was a completely unreasonable request. But I pointed out that I'd never asked for much, from him or anyone. I'd always been a self-cleaning oven. And I was ready to cash in the goodwill I'd built up through decades of forbearance for those two days with David.

The muses handed me argument after argument in defense of my request that I not have to say what I wanted or didn't want or would do or wouldn't do. I requested two days of intercalated time—a break from the ordinary scheme of things. I sold it like I was looking for angel investors in my tech start-up.

To my surprise and delight, my impassioned Power-Point sales deck and third-quarter projections worked.

Paul said, "Okay. Fair. Go with God."

It made me love him more.

When I thought of David, I was so discombobulated that I felt feral. On my way to a teaching gig, I felt heat spreading outward through the lower half of my body. I looked down to see if my period had come early and extra heavy, or if perhaps I was hemorrhaging to death. I expected to see my clothes soaking through with blood. But no. My dress was spotless. It wasn't blood—it was heat. Warmth being generated by my own body, warming me up like a space heater.

Leonard Cohen wrote that the only way to avoid sea-sickness is to become the ocean. I'd originally heard the line as "*becalm* the ocean," and I had no idea how I was going to go about making the ocean calm. When I heard it the right way, I thought, oh, *becoming* the ocean; that's no problem.

SIXTEEN

Sacred Waiting

When my mother's all-time favorite cat, an incredible mouser, vanished, Veronica said, "No, he didn't get eaten by coyotes! He just killed a deer and is dragging it down a mountain. It will take him awhile. Maybe many years."

I tried to imagine that what I longed for with David was coming for me, that it was just dragging a deer down the mountain. The waiting could be constructive. That way the good fortune would be even sweeter when it finally arrived. And yet, the weeks of waiting to see David after we'd made plans to meet in California were the most agonizing of my life.

I tried everything to distract and calm myself, including going to church. As part of his sermon, the priest told a version of the 1885 Leo Tolstoy short story "Where Love Is, God Is." I hadn't heard it before.

One night a cobbler heard Jesus say to him: "Look out onto the street tomorrow. I will come."

The next day, the cobbler stared out the window waiting for Jesus. As he did, he noticed an old man in the snow. He invited him in for tea and gave him warm clothes.

Later he saw a young woman and her baby freezing and brought them inside, played with the baby so the mother could rest, fed them and helped bundle them up against the cold.

Then he saw an old woman beating a boy for stealing an apple from her. He ran out, helped them make peace, and by the time they left, the boy was helping the old woman with her cart.

At the end of the day, the cobbler was disappointed that Jesus hadn't come, but in a dream he heard, "Did you not recognize me? I was hungry and you gave me food. I was thirsty and you gave me drink. I was a stranger and you welcomed me."

The promise had been kept, but at an hour and in a way that the cobbler did not expect.

I needed to look at the ways in which what I was waiting for had already arrived. I needed to learn how, at the very least, to make my yearning productive. German theologian Dietrich Bonhoeffer wrote, "The celebration of Advent is possible only to those who are troubled in soul, who know themselves to be poor and imperfect, and who look forward to something greater to come."

To help us tolerate the time apart, David suggested we create our own Advent calendar to cover the fifty days until we would see each other. Over those weeks we sent songs, stories, photos, interviews, letters. On Day 14, I told David about how I'd come to understand Emerson's analogy of the "transparent eyeball"; he sent me photos of his grandparents. On Day 18, I sent him "Eternal Flame" by the Bangles, and he told me about William and Henry James's cousin Minny Temple. William had said she was "a most honest little phenomenon, and there is a true respectability in the courage with which she keeps 'true to her own instincts.'"

On Day 27, I summarized the books of 1940s fashion designer Elizabeth Hawes: *Fashion Is Spinach*; *Why Women Cry: or Wenches with Wrenches*; *Hurry Up Please, It's Time*. I told him how she cut dresses on the bias and drank herself to death in the Chelsea Hotel in 1971. On that day he sent me the wedding vows his friends had written; he'd officiated.

On other days I offered thoughts on Madeleine L'Engle's car accident, Erasure's "Oh, L'Amour," a kitchen gadget called the egg cuber, the saint Padre Pio, the musical

Gypsy, and issues of *FATE* magazine. He sent aphorisms from *The Huainanzi* ("A standing wall is better once it topples; how much better if it had never been built"); theology from Jacob Boehme ("The hunger of the Soul must be turned to the source of eternal joy"), and sultry confessions ("The book I'd really like for us to write is a version of Aristotle's brilliant volume *Problems*"). We were with references like sharks are with blood in the water, snatching and tearing, smearing ourselves with words and sounds—and learning how to see the world through each other's eyes. We riffed off the table of contents for Nietzsche's *Ecce Homo*: "Why I Am So Wise, Why I Am So Clever, Why I Write Such Good Books, Why I Am a Destiny." Why Were We So Wise. Why Were We So Clever. Why Were We So Hilarious.

Even though we talked every day, all day, I ached for him. I still believed that one day the passion for David would play itself out and that if we did it right we'd maintain a friendship in books and letters, protect my marriage, find the elusive way between courting divorce and abandoning love. It was risky, but not to see him felt like a kind of death. David's Day 45 contribution, from Graham Greene: "I had to touch you with my hands, I had to taste you with my tongue; one can't love and do nothing."

SEVENTEEN

The Late Night

A s the trip to see David approached, Paul started going out rather often with women he knew. One night he met up with a female friend at seven p.m. That day had been busy. I'd volunteered at John's food pantry and then spent a few hours at the library. Once home I took a bath, cleaned the bathroom, did laundry, washed the dishes, listened to a whole audiobook on double speed, fed Nate dinner, vacuumed and mopped, ate a bowl of grapes. By this point it was eleven p.m.

I fully intended to stay married to Paul. I didn't want to lose him. He was faithful. There was no reason not to trust whatever he told me. Besides, I figured I would have to let Paul do whatever would make him feel better about my being alone with David. Though I did wonder if expansion without contraction was sustainable. I thought of the cliché about how staying married forever meant never wanting to get divorced at the same time. Was that going to be a problem for us, that I was yearning for someone else, and if he started doing that too we'd collapse? Or would we struggle either way, and if he also had someone else he'd feel more dignified?

Midnight. He still wasn't home. I frowned at the clock. I'd been cast in a role for which I had never auditioned. There was nothing uglier to me than jealousy, but here I was playing the Jealous Wife. I was angry at myself for feeling that way. And embarrassed too. How could I care what he did when I was full of desire for another man? I had no moral high ground. I shouldn't have been so upset, and yet I was.

So whose job was it to cure me of this suffering? Was it his job not to give me cause to feel jealous, or mine to learn how not to feel it? As Veronica liked to say, "Where does your neurosis end and his bad behavior start?" I longed to be so pure of heart that I'd be like the rabbi who ran after someone who'd stolen his wallet—not to get it back but to yell, "You can't steal that from me! It's a gift! I hope you enjoy it!"

Like a soldier praying in a trench, I picked up *Polysecure*.

The book began with a discussion of attachment theory, developed by British psychologist John Bowlby in the 1960s. I did the quizzes and realized I related to the "fearful-avoidant" attachment style. The principles of consensual nonmonogamy struck me as deeply reasonable: "love is not possessive or a finite resource; it is normal to be attracted to more than one person at the same time; there are multiple ways to practice love, sexual and intimate relationships; and jealousy is *not* something to be avoided or feared, but something that can be informative and worked through."

I respected the work. But I saw myself in the line: "It is not uncommon for me to hear people say that they theoretically want to be poly, but emotionally they don't know if they can do it because they feel like they are losing their mind." I didn't want to "rewire my triggers," or learn about "trigger contagion," or explore my "cycles of reactivity." I just didn't want Paul to have sex with other people, and I wanted to keep the other man I loved close. Was that too much to ask? Obviously.

The book's charts about what kind of relationships were where on the spectrum of open to closed made my head spin. I felt like all the writing about polyamory and swinging and the rest were insufficient when it came to how totally out of control I now felt in the face of love.

From the book—and really, was Paul still at the bar?—
I learned the ways in which having more than one lover
is, as therapists might say, complexifying. When our partner turns toward someone else—even with our knowledge or consent—it can start to feel very bad very fast.

Attraction to multiple people at the same time outside
of the emotional Thunderdome of Bachelor Nation feels
surreal. I wanted to be a good polyamory disciple, but I
kept pushing back on every lesson like a petulant student
in the last row rolling my eyes at everything the professor says.

Twelve thirty a.m. I'd never in my life done this, but I
texted Paul to ask if he was coming home. He'd been at
the bar with that woman, if they were still there, for six
hours. I was relieved when several minutes later he wrote
back and said yes, they were wrapping up, he'd be home
soon. The bar was a five-minute walk away. I wondered
if I should go there. Then I realized my dignity was more
valuable to me than knowing what was happening.

At one thirty a.m., when he still wasn't home, I started
physically shaking. I entered what I'd learned to call the
trauma vortex of abandonment terror. I broke out in a
cold sweat, the kind you get when you see a tiger in the
jungle. I was sure I smelled like fear. Insecurity pulled
me into a ditch like a blown tire.

I continued to read about attachment, and how to calm down when you start to panic. I tried to self-soothe. Still, I felt like I had to *do* something, only I didn't know what it was. I started throwing books into bags. When Paul walked in the door at about two, baffled to find me upset, I was furiously packing and trying to decide where I was going to go, if I was going to have to start over in a new city, if . . .

He said I was acting crazy. He'd stayed out that late a thousand times. Nothing had happened with the woman. After I'd texted, he'd gone to the bathroom and come back to find out they'd been given free drinks by the bartender, and his friend had started telling a long and involved personal story. He'd felt like it would have been rude to tear himself away.

EIGHTEEN

Whatever We Do

Bleak House of Boning, The War and Peace of Dick, My Polysecure Struggle . . . " Paul started joking that I should write an eight-hundred-page book about being in an open marriage. I admired his ability to overcome jealousy through levity even as I flinched at crass words like "boning" to describe something that felt so pure.

If there was a story in any of this, I felt like it was how David and I had unlocked something in each other, something that felt unstoppable. I wanted to merge with him in every way possible.

I had voices in my head asking me if I was deluding myself. I knew that the story of every affair is always about how "This is different! This love is like no other!" People explode their lives and then so often a few years later they say, "Never mind! It wasn't different after all," and leave that person too.

Every time I saw anything online about how someone was with one person and fell in love with another, I noticed they were crucified. "I wish the worst for you both," a colleague had posted under a podcast about a couple who left their spouses for each other. "You're going to fail and I'm going to laugh," wrote another. A third: "Love and sex aren't sacred and beautiful and you're not a special snowflake who gets to have that. What you have is a brief infatuation. Just you wait. Any day now you'll be back here trudging through life and loneliness like the rest of us."

Seeing those reactions was chilling, but I didn't think they applied to me. For one thing, as long as I wasn't lying, I wasn't cheating. Paul and I were figuring it out together. And I had full faith that even though it was difficult I would find a way to preserve my marriage, to keep my family from the violence of a divorce. With enough thoughtfulness and work, I could incorporate David into my life in a safe way that would benefit everyone.

Usually, Paul agreed. He said that the challenge was just to embrace the notion of "liminal relationships." He began to describe us to his friends, with pride, as practicing "consensual nonmonogamy." He didn't want them to think I was having a secret affair, which would be emasculating.

"Affairs love vagueness," he said. "They love the dark, like mold and potatoes." He preferred the antiseptic light of *Polysecure*. I struggled with the labels and began to joke that what we were practicing was "grudging nonmonogamy." And I didn't want people to know, so I hoped it would also be "top-secret nonmonogamy."

To show my commitment to the marriage, I took Paul out for a date night. As we settled into an outdoor table under a wooden framework decorated with fake flowers he said, "Do you feel open to hearing some things about me and other people? We've talked a lot about your desires but not as much about mine."

"Sure," I said. I was feeling strong, and I had a very full glass of red wine in front of me. The weather was crisp. A heater hummed above us.

"I have something to confess," he said.

"Is this about the night when you were out late?" I said.

"No, nothing actually happened that night. We were just drinking a lot. It's about something a long time ago."

"Go ahead," I said.

"You know how I've always said that Sarah and I had an emotional affair?"

"Yes."

"Well, it was more than that."

I felt my body sink as if its mass had doubled. Gravity changed the way it did at the Planetarium when you went from one scale to another and learned that on Venus you might weigh 149 pounds whereas on the moon you'd be just 27. Where was I now? Whatever part of the universe had the most gravity. A neutron star?

Now that I was being pulled to the center of the earth by the force of twenty-three trillion pounds, I had to work to blink as if opening and closing an iron gate. But I forced myself not to cry. I began to ask questions in a detached and curious way, as one might ask new friends about how they decorated their house.

"I'd sort of thought that might be true, but I didn't really want to know," I said. "Did you sleep with her?"

"Yes."

While I'd always suspected it, this news mattered, the way when someone dies everything is different even if the patient had been sick for years. I took a long drink of my wine. "How many times?"

"A few."

I wasn't sure what I expected to hear—once, maybe.

"Over how long a period?"

"A couple of months."

Images floated into my mind. They were devouring each other on beds, on couches, against walls. His muscular back with her thin, shapely legs wrapped around him . . .

"Where?"

"At her apartment."

"What else?"

"I made out with Jacqueline one night at a bar and on the street another time."

"Anything else?"

"Yes," he said. He described a few other moments of infidelity, mostly with people I knew vaguely and who it had never occurred to me he could like.

I was quiet for a minute. For many years, in spite of my suspicions, I'd believed what he'd told me. I'd used the term "emotional affair" in speaking to others about his relationship with Sarah. I'd said it with something like smugness. *When you say "affair," you mean husbands who have sex with other women. But my husband loves me, loves our family, too much to do that, so he just wants to, but doesn't.*

Even without an acknowledged sexual component that relationship with Sarah had been rough on us. But he'd relinquished her, suffered, and our relationship had grown stronger as we raised our son together all those years.

"I'm sorry," he said. "I didn't believe in you or myself enough to tell you before now."

I looked around and was surprised to find that the restaurant was the same as it had been an hour earlier. Then I realized that I felt something like relief. This news was terrible in so many ways, but in at least one it was *fantastic*. I was in love with someone else and yet *Paul* was apologizing to *me*.

"Thank you for lying to me," I said. "If I'd known at the time, I would have divorced you and then we wouldn't have raised our kid together, and I'm glad we did. I forgive you."

Then it was my turn to come clean—only I had no secrets of my own to reveal because I'd never kept any. I was glad to know the truth about his past. For one thing, I felt that his having had sex with someone else without my saying it was okay gave me cover for possibly having sex with someone else when he'd said it was fine.

He'd betrayed me and then lied about it. Whatever was happening with David, I wasn't being reckless. David and I had not even kissed. We wanted each other, but we hadn't decided yet if we'd do anything about it. We were trying to be extremely deliberate, not break anything. And now I knew that even if I did sleep with him, I wasn't drawing first blood in my marriage. My sense of righteousness was a bit pathetic, but there it was.

Veronica had said what David and I had was "platonic

love with erotic edges," that Paul and I were doing the hard work of trying to make "a thoughtful exception to monogamy." But she did warn me that if I slept with David all bets were off. She said that the volatility of the situation had brought out an aggressive energy in Paul and that staying out late at bars with women without telling me when he'd be home might be the tip of a chaos iceberg.

On the way home after our dinner, Paul asked me what was new with David. He remained eager to make the connection be about sex, not love. The contrast between how he spoke about it and how it felt was jarring.

"Is he sending you dick pix?" Paul asked.

"No!" I said, horrified that he thought that was something he or I would do.

"How do you flirt?"

"We send each other books?" I said. "Maybe sort of: 'Check out this poem from the thirteenth century. Here's a song from when I was a little kid.'" I told him about *Zoo*.

He seemed disappointed.

In the days that followed, the revelation about his affair hit me harder than I'd realized at the time. It was like discovering injuries after an accident's been cleared and you've walked away patting yourself, crowing, "No broken bones!"

Something about the long deception had me rethinking things I thought I'd known. I'd trusted my husband. He had deceived me. How much did I care about having been duped? Was I grateful about being lied to or was I furious? And why, again, was I hesitating for a second to spend time with David given this new data point?

I didn't quite know how to explain how much chemistry David and I had, how good—deeply good—it felt to share things with each other. I thought of the Lucinda Williams song "Something About What Happens When We Talk." It felt like we had created our own language.

I recalled someone who worked at the Museum of Modern Art talking about how the poets Frank O'Hara and John Ashbery discussed their work with each other. Ashbery said, "Do you think there's too much gold in my poem?" and O'Hara said, "No, darling, I think it's very *summery*." The curator thought, *"My God, what kind of literary criticism is this anyway?"*

I imagined someone overhearing David and me and them feeling the same way: *What kind of conversation is this anyway? They're just staring at each other and occasionally quoting Emerson. I mean, Pillow Books and Choose Your Own Adventures? Can't they just screw around like normal people?*

We kept saying we weren't sure if our relationship would be physical, but it felt as though we were playing out a game of Clue even though we'd already seen the solution in the center of the board—and it was more art-house film than family-friendly board game.

For my final Advent calendar submission, I pretended to be Abelard arguing against our kissing, though I admittedly picked all the weakest dodgeball players for that team. He replied with a long letter as Heloise arguing for our making out. His dialogue incorporated three languages and a dozen footnotes. In the end, he quoted Saint Augustine: "Give me chastity and continence—but not yet."

NINETEEN

Just French

T hanks to the constant stream of emails from David, each night I fell asleep full of new ideas and images and questions. By the side of my bed were stacks of books—C. S. Lewis, Wordsworth, Wallace Stevens. I felt happy to be alive. There was something about all of this that felt like paradise. Still, paradise was not my only home.

The day before my trip, while Nate was out with friends, Paul and I took a long walk. He told me how he wanted an open marriage to work even though he was struggling with the intensity of the relationship I had with David. The solution he'd come up with: he wanted to go all in on the embracing-the-world action, which might involve his doing things like online dating and going dancing in nightclubs, something he missed that I never wanted to do. He asked me if I could see the beauty in that.

Frankly, I could not see the holiness in what felt like hedonism for its own sake. I tried to be a good sport and to ask questions rather than sharing my discomfort, but the conversation quickly grew tense. We began discussing the online-dating question with a commitment to dialogue rarely seen outside of model UN.

"I mean, I need to do *something*," he said. "When you're off with someone else I can't sit idly by."

"Sure you can," I said. "Have you tried it?"

"I can't tell if you're joking," he said.

"Okay, so let's play this out," I said. "Say you're really doing this. Are you going to start running around with much younger women? What age will you set as the low end?"

"Half my age plus seven is the rule."

"What rule?" I said. "Says who?"

"Everyone," he said, as if I were an idiot for not knowing.

As we were fighting our way down the sidewalk, Paul accidentally tripped me.

"I had to walk in front of you because that guy was about to bump into me!" he said as I regained my footing.

"When someone falls down, you say, 'Are you okay?' first!" I shouted. "Only then do you start making excuses!"

We kept walking and talking in circles. After about three hours of this, I became so overwhelmed that I asked to take a break and be alone for a bit. He said, "You always do that—bail just when we're about to have a breakthrough."

I didn't like to think of myself that way, so I agreed to keep walking. But a few blocks later I said I really did need a break. He said, "Just a bit more." A couple of minutes after that I yelled, far louder and shriller than I meant to, "I said I needed a *break*!" and threw my keys on the ground.

People eating brunch at an outdoor café looked up in alarm. I picked up my keys and stormed off. Paul later said everyone looked at him like he'd hit me. We avoided each other for the rest of the day. That morning I'd felt good about everything. By the time I went to bed he was at a show with a friend, and I was wishing he'd stay gone.

Veronica said it was time to set some clear boundaries, to give each relationship a meaningful shape: "Paul is your husband. David is your second half. Nothing should make you turn your back on a soulmate if you're lucky enough to find him. If you have the capacity to maintain both relationships, why wouldn't you? Here's a question to ask yourself: What do you know for sure?"

"I know I don't want my kid to come from divorced

parents," I said. "I love Paul. I am in love with David. If my father died then I'd want them both at the funeral."

"What you want is not so insane," she said, "just French."

Veronica added that the key was to be honest and open about the reality and our expectations. So, to say to Paul, for example: "We're ride-or-die. We've been together a long time and really worked out how to be with each other. This relationship has value. You're my best friend, we have a great family, we sleep together. I have another man in my life, and you can have people on the side too. And we also have to treat each other with respect. For instance, you have to call me if you're going to be out late. I can learn to be okay with you having a girlfriend, but not with you being unreliable."

I said I wasn't sure if I could tolerate his having other partners.

"You could handle it," she said. "If he was respectful and kind about it, it could be okay. One thing, though, that's good to keep in mind, is that love is infinite but time and energy aren't."

She recalled a time in college when she'd had two boyfriends at the same time. They both sat in the waiting room when she had her wisdom teeth out. When she looked back on that, she remembered feeling very loved. "It was messy and everyone cried a lot, but I'm not sorry. I don't think love is bad, ever. I've known you since we were eight. You've been looking for this kind of spiritual connection your whole life. You raised your child. You took care of everyone else. Now you get to be happy."

My eyes filled with tears so quickly that I thought back to *Zoo*, one of the first things David and I read together. In that book the character weeps "not out of sentimentality, but the way windows weep in a room heated for the first time in many weeks."

In the prior weeks, there had been days when I'd thought maybe I should not go to California after all. It would be better for everyone if we stayed on the astral plane. Then the next day I'd found myself at the library so undone by longing for David that I could not concentrate. I'd been coursing with energy for as long as we'd been talking, but something had changed. Ever since I'd booked my trip I'd been half there in my head—sitting with him on a couch, feeling his weight beside me, my hand unbuttoning the top button of his shirt. And then the day came.

TWENTY

California

Twenty minutes before landing, I felt that my heart might shoot out of my chest and onto the tarmac, and I worried that I'd given myself food poisoning with the airport wrap I'd had to make myself eat. I couldn't believe I was actually about to get what I wanted. I wondered what it would be like.

David and I would have our own rooms. We had no plans for our two days together. I thought we might be so shell-shocked that we would just stare at each other for forty-eight hours. When my plane landed, I texted him to let him know. He said he thought that he might faint.

We'd been talking every day and had exchanged more than four hundred thousand words. When he expressed his love for me on the page, he'd said, "These are words

I've never spoken and they are words you've never heard, trust me." I felt it to be true.

Frances McDormand said once in an interview that the way to ensure a long relationship was to wait for everything to build up so you couldn't stand it anymore: "Keep it across the room for as long as you can." Given how consumed we were, my thinking was *we should not keep it across the room a second longer.*

Later that day, I opened the door to my room and David stepped inside. I froze. He was a real person. I couldn't quite believe it. He seemed completely foreign to me and also like my twin. For all we'd written, in each other's presence we were speechless.

We hugged tightly. And then, my right hand, independent of any direction from my brain, reached up and gently took hold of the left collar of his shirt. As I pulled him toward me I was met with the same resistance you'd get from ripe fruit coming off the branch. I felt that we were doing what we were put on earth to do. I put his strong hand on my hip, and he held it there. I could feel his fingers grabbing and releasing through my skirt. I wanted to live inside that kiss, to kiss him every second for the rest of my life.

Then, without a word or any conscious thought, we were naked. His body was so sturdy; his arms and his back and his calves—every inch was a delightful surprise. We fit together like a key in a lock. For the first time in my life I understood what it meant to become one flesh.

He looked into my eyes, and I looked back into his, an infinity symbol of regard. With each touch, he made me feel safe and held. *What are we doing?* I thought. The answer came back: *We are* loving *each other.* That was the feeling I had: of loving and being loved. I'd never experienced sex quite like that before. No one had ever done that to me or asked that of me. It felt like deliverance.

We stayed in that bed as the light changed outside and we could see the moon. Eventually, astonished, we began talking.

"Who are you?" he said finally, breaking the silence. "I can't believe you're here. I can't believe you're real."

We wondered if we should go out and get dinner. Then we stayed in bed. We talked about our lives and books. I pulled him onto me again and admired how our bodies looked, together at last.

"When it comes to your next project, I really think you should consider Petrarch," he said, pausing on top of me. "Petrarch didn't write for his contemporaries; he wrote for future generations. What book would you write if you took ten years to write it? If you weren't lending out your talent for other people's books?"

I looked back into his eyes. His brow was slightly furrowed. He was so sincere and so sweet, so determined. I thought of the notes I'd seen about him on a professor-rating website, and I agreed with all the students who'd described him as one of those teachers who really *cares*. He somehow made me feel perfect while revealing ways in which I could become better.

David patiently waited for me to reply, as if he'd asked me for the answer to a question that he'd been preparing me to answer all semester.

"Consider *Petrarch*?" I said. "Are you giving me an assignment *while you're inside me*?"

"Yes, sorry," he said and laughed. "But I mean it. In *Letters to Posterity* he—"

I kissed him so he'd stop talking. I pulled him deeper into me. We didn't have to read anymore or write anymore. Now we were the poem.

I'd been having sex for decades by that point. I thought I was good at it. I would have said before that moment that I'd had plenty of good sex. And yet on that day, it felt as though I were doing everything for the first time. Except for short forays out for coffee or food we stayed in bed for two days straight. The entire time I felt drunk even though we hadn't had any alcohol.

As I rested with my head on his chest, he kept talking to me quietly as my eyes closed in spite of my trying to keep them open. I startled awake a few minutes later. "Wait!" I cried, lifting myself up in bed. "I fell asleep. What did I miss?"

"Just the *Ecce Homo* table of contents," he said. "Why you are so wise, why you are so clever, why you are a destiny . . ."

The next morning, we woke up before dawn. He grabbed a book from the bedside table and read me Whitman until I distracted him. He threw the book on the floor. Once we'd made love a final time, he went back to reading. As he reached Section 50 of the poem, I felt like I'd been placed at the top of a cliff and given a nudge.

Something it swings on more than the earth I swing on,

To it the creation is the friend whose embracing awakes me.

Perhaps I might tell more. Outlines! I plead for my brothers and sisters.

Do you see O my brothers and sisters?

It is not chaos or death—it is form, union, plan—it is eternal life—it is

Happiness.

The cool air coming through the window lifts the drapes in the rhythm to a song I can suddenly hear. Every sound and smell is telling the same story, and my body is reading it out loud while writing it. Every hair on my body stands up, straining to hear the next line.

My breath, his breath, the fan all breathe in and out together, rising and falling. The bed is made of moss, the sheets giant green leaves, as alive as we are. The ceiling is a dark blue sky turning pink and purple. His body and mine are performing a ritual. We're sliding along slippery rocks in a cool river, dipping under the surface.

Memories pass through me like a current, of nursing, climbing the park jungle gym as a little girl, passing notes in class, holding a friend while she cried. I'm praying; no, I am the prayer.

David is here and I'm alone, everyone who ever lived and no one. Outside, I hear women walking to work, heels against the sidewalk; angry drivers backing up trucks; serious birds chirping. They're out there, not knowing that inside this room the world is coming to its conclusion. David and I, buried in one grave, born into the world, giving birth to it.

My grandmother never had this, I think—I don't think; I know. Because here she is with me, telling me it's true; she never had a man kiss her like this, read her poetry while the sun came up, look into her soul in a bedroom's half-light.

When whatever happened stopped happening, I looked at David.

"Did you feel that?" I asked him.

"Yes," he said. He looked as dazed as I felt.

I got up. In the bathroom mirror I was surprised to find myself still there. Had that moment lasted minutes or days? The streetlights outside the window had gone out; the sun was coming up. My eyes were dilated. I could have died that day.

TWENTY-ONE

The Drop

On March 18, 1958, theologian Thomas Merton had a mystical experience: "In Louisville, at the corner of Fourth and Walnut, in the center of the shopping district, I was suddenly overwhelmed with the realization that I loved all those people, that they were mine and I was theirs, that we could not be alien to one another even though we were total strangers. . . . There is no way of telling people that they are all walking around shining like the sun."

There was no way of telling people what I'd seen and felt, but I thought of nothing else. I'd brought the paperback edition of Whitman back with me from California. I carried it everywhere like a flower I'd plucked in a dream and found myself holding when I woke up. I had been transformed. How was it possible no one else could tell?

Back home, I tried to resume my old life, but everything felt wrong. Before California all I could think about was being with David. Everything beyond that had been the map of a flat earth; the ships sailed right off the edge. I gazed at the photos we'd taken on that trip like they were of my new baby and I'd waited my whole life to have a child.

But now I felt as though that child had been taken away. When the First Great Awakening ended, Jonathan Edwards said there was a sense that God was withdrawing and Satan was rushing in to fill the void: "Some pious persons . . . had it urged upon them as if somebody had spoke to them, *Cut your throat, now is a good opportunity. Now! Now!*"

David and I had agreed that we'd take the sublimation route going forward. We felt lucky to have had so much already. But the world didn't make sense without him. The world didn't make sense anymore, period. I felt like I'd died, and no one had noticed.

In the shower, I left deep conditioner in my hair for three minutes like I was supposed to, to combat frizziness. Frizziness was a problem in the right-side-up world, I recalled. I felt like the alien Jeff Bridges played in the

'80s movie *Starman*, trying to make sense of earth culture. When I received a text from a colleague, I pressed the button that made the "ha-ha" hover over her words, because I seemed to recall that was how human beings interacted. Every minute that I wasn't proclaiming the Truth of the divine among us felt like a lie. I felt new sympathy for street-corner preachers. I didn't understand what had happened, but to quote Pascal, "Everything that is incomprehensible does not cease to exist."

Contact with the unexplained did not feel like particularly good news for me. When I worked at a music magazine, my nerdy boss, on whom I had a mad crush, said of Gloria Gaynor, "Finding God was a bad career move." I began to suspect that having a religious experience had ended my hit-making days too. I didn't know that I'd ever write another book, because how could I put any of this into words? And what else was worth talking about?

For a long time now, women friends, once we were alone, had confided that at night they stared at the ceiling asking questions about what came next and why it could all feel so hard. When I validated their feelings, they'd say: "Yes, that's *why* it's hard, but what's the *answer*?"

They wanted a mantra, a supplement, a club, something concrete and actionable. I'd wanted to give it to them, but I had always come up short. I would offer thoughts on our problems and discuss the value of community, the latest research on hormones, and how to find meaning in the stories of our lives. But now I had a new answer, and it was inconvenient.

"You're not going to like it," I imagined myself telling my friends as I looked into their hopeful, tired faces. "The answer is love. Wait, maybe God? No, it's love! I think they could be the same. How do you find it? I think . . . fall madly in love with a friend and go to the library?"

Maybe wanting life to feel true and vibrant wasn't a generational, financial, or physical challenge but a spiritual one. Any spiritual path would do, probably. And yet, I would tell my peers that, while falling in love with someone new and wonderful would certainly distract you from your misery, it would also create a sense of disorientation so profound that you would float down supermarket aisles like a phantom.

What I felt was *aporia*, an immobilized confusion so great I needed a Greek word for it. Getting groceries, I looked around the store and felt like I didn't belong there, as I didn't belong anywhere. I stood staring at the different jams and jellies for what felt like a hundred years. I stayed there the entire length of the Gin Blossoms song "Til I Hear It from You" playing over the store's sound system, tears rolling down my cheeks. I'd been in the Garden of Eden, and I'd been cast out, forced to roam and suffer.

They say crying clears out the residue of what was there before. When you're disoriented, crying is a proper response. But what about when you can't *stop*? What about when you dissolve into a puddle that needs to be mopped up by cheerful stockers in Hawaiian shirts?

I felt dead. Only I felt like a graveside mourner too. I kept switching roles, the way I had at times in a moment of orgasm, sexual situations flashing through my brain, only this version was depressing. Now I was the corpse and the doctor and the widow, the candy striper who asks the grieving family if she can get them anything and the *We're losing her, doctor!* nurse. The medical examiner leaning against the morgue bay after a long day of autopsies. "Love killed her," he says, snapping off his gloves.

"You're really sad, aren't you?" David asked me in an email. "I didn't realize how sad you were."

For my birthday, he sent me an audio file of him reading Whitman's "Song of Myself" Section 50. I walked around the park near the library listening to it. As I had in that hotel room, I felt my soul lifting out of my body.

On a voicemail he said, "We have an ability to bring something out in each other, to be so truly ourselves." He seemed clear that the struggle in that poem would manifest itself in our lives, and he seemed confident that it was necessary. "The struggle is good," he said.

It sure doesn't feel *good*, I thought.

Still, it didn't feel *wrong*. In one way, everything felt righter than it ever had. Maybe goodness didn't matter so much. Maybe love was beyond good and evil. "There is no problem of evil," wrote musician Nick Cave. "There is only a problem of good. Why does a world that is so often cruel insist on being beautiful, of being good? Why does it take a devastation for the world to reveal its true spiritual nature?"

I got COVID for the first time and spent a week in bed trying to work on my laptop even as I coughed and faded in and out of sleep. When I was awake, I tried watching television, but everything made me cry. When Mariska Hargitay caught a bad guy on *Law & Order: SVU*, I cried. When someone in the military came home in a commercial, I cried. When the French election results were called, I was moved to tears by how European television revealed the results via holograms of the presidents appearing Spock-like inside the Élysée Palace. When I texted Helen, she wrote back to say that she was concerned—it was not a good sign that I was now weeping over "white guys teleporting into a grand palais."

I listened to a podcast that called a low time after a peak experience "the drop." If that's what this was then it was not a dip in the road but a roller coaster with a hyperbolic name and ride-along videos on YouTube.

While I had COVID, Paul and I fought as we'd never fought before. I thought he should bring me water without my having to ask. Every time I felt upset with him it brought up other areas in which I felt that we were out of balance.

I was working so hard so I could be allowed to spend those two days with the man I'd fallen in love with one time before sacrificing him on the altar of our marriage. And I'd made even that sound sexy for Paul even though it was sacred. Paul woke me up in the night asking for reassurance. He would storm out the door and go for walks alone and then come back and glower and tell me I didn't appreciate him enough.

"You're selfish now," he said. "This is the snapback after a lifetime of being a good girl. You want everything and you feel you deserve it. You're asking too much of me. I've had to share you with everyone—the boy, your friends, your parents. David pushes me to the limit. When do I get your time and energy?"

CRUSH

Maybe I'd have more time and energy if you did more work, I thought but did not say.

When he felt more playful, he asked: "What's it like getting to sleep with two people without getting in trouble?"

Oh, I'm in trouble, I thought.

The truth was that sleeping with two men in a short span of time felt weird. *I should feel lucky*, I thought. But I just felt sad and confused. Love triangles looked entertaining from afar. I tried to think of myself as Archie, and these two men as Betty and Veronica; or as Bella, and the men as the sexy vampire and the sexy werewolf, the three of us trapped in a cycle of lust. But I couldn't find solace in any cartoonish narratives.

Paul was relieved that the situation with David was theoretically over now and we could get back to our lives as they'd been before. When he noticed how mournful I was, he said, "You cry at the cast party whether the play you were in was great or terrible. People think the only beautiful things are the permanent ones, but the ephemeral can be beautiful too. That's how shows are for me."

I hated that he was trying to reduce what had happened to me to one of his friends' productions. No one could relate to what had happened to me.

Still delirious as the line on the test strips began to turn faint, I pulled myself out of bed and went and sat alone,

159

masked, in the park by the river. A woman walking her rheumy-eyed sheepdog yelled, "No! She's wearing black!" I looked up in alarm. She said, "The dog was heading your way. I didn't want him to mess up your clothes. The fur gets everywhere."

I cried because she was being so thoughtful.

TWENTY-TWO

Lucid Dreaming

One night Paul and I were watching TV when the main character yelled at her sister's husband, after he's lost his family and his dignity and is living in a run-down motel: "How could you cheat on my sister? How could you be so stupid?"

Right. That's what the world would say about all this. So stupid! Of course. There was no plan for me to see David again. I mourned him more than I'd ever mourned any loss in my life.

Paul and I had teary, all-night conversations in which he said he couldn't handle it if I loved David and slept with him again too.

"I might be able to handle one, but I certainly can't handle both," he said.

"We're not going to sleep together again," I said.

"Don't act like that makes you a martyr," he said. "I'm your husband, not him. This was always supposed to be something good for us, not only for you."

He needed me to say I still loved him and would never leave him. I said all the right things, but I didn't feel them.

What I felt was claustrophobic. Paul was always *there*. I took on extra work and spent many hours each day on my laptop, with him sitting three feet away. I overper-formed my role at home. I cleaned out the fridge drawers with bleach. I organized Nate's shelves. I baked a plum torte.

One day Veronica called as I was leaving the drugstore carrying two large bags and a new mop. I awkwardly carried the bags and the mop all over the neighborhood while on the phone. I hadn't spoken with her in a while, and she asked if I'd been mad at her. I said no—I'd just been afraid to talk to her because I wasn't sure how she'd react to my sleeping with David, or to the news of my mystical experience. I'd feared she might judge or doubt me in some way that I couldn't handle yet.

She said, "Don't you know by now that you could kill someone, and I'd only want to know how you felt about it?"

CRUSH

"How long will I be sad?" I asked.

"If you work very hard on feeling better, a month and a half. And if you do nothing, thirty-two years."

"I have to get some time alone," I said. "But Paul's going to want to go with me."

"I'm going to the library," I said when I got home.

"I'll come with you!" Paul said.

I didn't feel like I could say no. As we walked, he asked yet again for reassurance.

"We'll always be together, right?"

"Right," I said. But the more he asked, the more my doubt grew. And the madder I got.

In the old days, wasn't the cliché that when a man worked hard, he got to have a mistress, and his wife took care of the kids and the house? But I did that too! And I was so *tired*. I started to envy people who were single or who were placidly content in their marriages. *They must sleep so well*, I thought.

I slept terribly, waking up every two hours in a flood of anxiety. To help fix the problem, I checked out a book on lucid dreaming, a psychological exercise designed to let you control your nocturnal life. The first night I tried it, my dreams became like on-demand movies. I swam in the ocean. I walked through forests.

Then the next I settled in for another meaningful,

163

restful dream. I was strolling through a meadow at sun-
rise, deer and rabbits loping around me, when I encountered a group of teenagers. I stopped to ask what wise
words they had to offer me. One picked up a branch and
hit me in the head. I fell into the dirt, and the rest of the
gang stomped on me. I tried to explain the concept of
lucid dreaming to them: I was in charge; they served me.
They laughed and hit me harder. I woke up in a sweat,
panting. I didn't try to practice lucid dreaming anymore
after that.

TWENTY-THREE

Effing the Ineffable

That time with David had changed everything. For as much as I'd been shaken up by falling in love and by the drama of an open marriage, I was undone most by what I considered a hierophany, the sacred breaking through into everyday human experience.

What did it mean? What were its implications? I'd been called to a new life, but I didn't know exactly what the call was or how to answer it. I tried very hard to make my new revelation fit into my old life, to do right by everyone I'd made promises to, to keep things just as they had been, even though nothing was the same.

I returned to some of the same books I'd read as a teenage seeker hoping for a vision, only now I was looking for an explanation of the one I'd had. I thought of how naïve I'd been to want this. I'd asked for it, then I'd gotten it. Now what?

Everyone, even William James in *The Varieties of Religious Experience*, seemed to agree that there was no easy way to talk about that sort of thing, that it was ineffable, and then they all went ahead and talked about it for hundreds of pages. I found myself underlining phrases like "the Initiation of Man into the Immemorial Mystery of the Open Secret of Being."

One of James's subjects talked about what he discovered coming out of anesthesia, that he emerged a half second before the spiral of time started back up again. He got to see "a glimpse of my heels, a glimpse of the eternal process just in the act of starting." Foreshadowing *Bill and Ted's Excellent Adventure*, James said one could encounter oneself in that moment: "You could kiss your own lips."

At the library I found a trove of mysticism books by Evelyn Underhill that I felt had been waiting in the stacks just for me for a hundred years, books with titles like *Practical Mysticism: A Little Book for Normal People*. A mystical experience involves a "violent shattering and rearranging of the self," she wrote. This allows you to "find yourself, literally, to be other than you were before."

I asked everyone I talked to if they'd ever had a mystical experience. A surprising number had, usually one or two times each. One woman told me that sitting on an airplane a few years earlier during a hard time in her life she'd suddenly been hit with a vision: "I went in and out of consciousness. I thought I might be dying. And I didn't think of my parents or my children. I just knew for a fact that I was alone in the universe but also not alone at all. The message that kept repeating was, 'Love—it's all love.'"

Another said that when she went to sit with grieving friends after another friend of theirs had died that there was a strange energy in the room, "like we were outside of time."

Walt Whitman kept showing up in my mysticism research. According to a book called *Ineffability*: "Whitman is an example of the prodigious desire for connection and for flooding of the channels."

I tried to remember the closest I'd come to feeling this way before, and the best I could do was four months into my pregnancy. The word "quickening" felt old-fashioned, but it was the only good word to describe that point when you know there is another *person* inside your body, and they're *moving around*. The only other word that approaches the feeling is "flutter."

I regretted that I hadn't pushed back harder when Paul said he didn't want more children. Now it was too late.

I'd had all the babies I'd ever have. From there on, I'd have to make do with giving Ring Pops and legwarmers and picture books to other people's daughters. That I'd never have a child with David struck me as the saddest thing in the world. I wondered if it meant anything that so many female saints seemed to have had their religious experiences at a stage in life when biological miracles aren't available anymore.

Talking to Veronica on the phone I said, "Let me read you this quote from Hildegard of Bingen: 'In the year 1142, when I was forty-two years and seven months old, it happened that a great light of brilliant fire came from the open heavens and overwhelmed all my mind, my heart, and my breast, not so much like a flickering flame, but rather like glowing heat, as the sun warms other things on which it sheds its rays.'

"And here's Saint Teresa of Avila: 'My soul suddenly became recollected and seemed to me to become bright all over like a mirror: no part of it—back, sides, top or bottom—but was completely bright.' Bertrand Russell—"

"Okay, enough!" Veronica said.

"I just want to know what it is I'm being called to do," I said. "Is the universe pointing at David, saying, 'Be with him'? Or am I just supposed to, like, *tithe*?"

As a teenager, I'd wanted to have a mystical experience. Now that I had, I learned epiphanies had consequences.

Sex was part but not all of what had happened. When I read the Song of Songs or books about kundalini awakening, I thought of David's strong hands on my hips pulling me toward him, of the way his mouth garlanded my neck in little bruises. I remembered him holding on to the headboard behind my head. Kissing me for hours, so hard my lip bled. Part of me had never left that bedroom. Part of me was there still, my skirt and his shirt balled up together on the floor.

And yet, whatever it was that had happened was not purely physical. That moment had changed me in a fundamental and permanent way.

In the day-to-day world of meal planning and deadlines, I kept my head down, worked hard, drank water, went for walks, filled the fridge with food for my family. Then one day on the way to a work meeting, I heard "Remember the Mountain Bed" come on in my headphones. Woody Guthrie's lyrics about a perfect physical and spiritual encounter transported me from a busy sidewalk to that California hotel room. I saw a plane in the sky and the wind kicked up and everything started to shimmer.

TWENTY-FOUR

Rendering Unto

I kept thinking about the biblical admonition to render unto Caesar what is Caesar's. My job now, I decided, was simply to give everyone what they were owed: Paul, David, Nate, the lady at the post office. To Paul I needed to show appreciation. And so I not only continued to sleep with him, but I also took him on a weekend trip. I wanted to prove that I was not withholding love from him to give it to someone else. Pacified and cared for, he said I should go ahead and see David again because he knew it would make me happy.

When he said that, I stopped crying every day. I reassured Paul that I didn't even need to be alone with David or to sleep with him, if I could only see him . . .

David came to town.

Walking to our meeting spot, I saw him from a great distance. He noticed me the second I noticed him. We smiled at each other and shook our heads in astonishment as we got closer and closer. We met at a crosswalk and held each other until a car came close and then we picked a side of the street. On the sidewalk, we stood looking at each other in awe, smiling and hugging.

Then we started wandering. I told him that I'd been given Paul's blessing to see him but that I thought we should try to segue now into a platonic friendship. He agreed, and said he was just so glad we'd get to see each other and talk.

For three hours, we caught each other up on our lives and walked through one neighborhood after another, barely noticing where we were. This was all we needed! A friendship! Closeness! And this wouldn't jeopardize my marriage. I wanted to kiss him, but I held myself back. We were learning to restrain ourselves. When we did, it felt like we'd passed a test. I left our walk proud, nourished, and sunburned.

Straight from there I went to see Paul for dinner. He was angry with me that I'd seen David, even though he'd known I was going to see him and had explicitly said it was fine. I thought he'd be pleased that we'd kept our hands off each other—didn't he like knowing that we could? But of course sex was never the problem, and so my decorum did not make him feel any better.

I asked him friendly questions, tried to keep it light, but he sulked as we sat down at an outdoor restaurant. He glared at me as British people chain-smoked next to us. He had the psychic energy of a troll under a bridge.

"Why are you in such a bad mood?" I asked.

"You've read a thousand books with David, and you can't finish the one book I asked you to read."

"Which book?"

"*Polysecure.*"

"I read some of it."

He glared at me. "When are you making space for what I want? When do I get to have some of the aliveness you have? When's it my turn?"

Your turn for the universe to reveal its glory to you in someone else's arms? Are you going to find your spiritual twin on Tinder? I thought. But instead of saying that, I said, "I'm sorry. I understand that you want more of my attention and for me to be more enthusiastic about your desire for other people. I'll do my best to get there."

When we got home, I opened up the book he wanted me to read, highlighter in hand. I learned that I should name my reactive self. Was I the Ice Queen, the Bolter, the Bulldog? I guessed Bolter because of the time I'd responded to his staying out late by flinging books into bags.

The book asked: "What is your reactivity protecting?"

Uh, vulnerability?

"What did the vulnerable part need?"

In my mind, I pronounced it with a *w* not a *v*, because one of Veronica's daughters was in a Latin summer program once that was extremely challenging. When we asked how she was, she said, because *v*'s are pronounced as *w*'s in Latin, "I'm feeling *wery wulnerable.*" Veronica and I immediately abandoned the correct pronunciation of the word and have used hers with each other ever since. All those years of *wulnerability.*

But back to my assignment! What was the cure for vulnerability?

Safety, connection, to be seen, to know you matter.

Where could I find that safety? How could I give that to myself and to Paul?

Nonmonogamy isn't so different from monogamy, the book argued. It just tends to amplify the problems that are there in any intimate relationship, the terror of loving and being loved. The challenge of any close relationship is to work through the fear and come out stronger.

"Because what you've done is the exception to the

rule, we have to think about the rule now," Paul said. "And if the rule bent for you it needs to bend for me. I'm not saying we have to have a coming-out party as non-monogamous with flags outside the house and promise rings for all our lovers, but I'd like some acknowledgment, some labeling. And I'd like people beyond just our friends to know what's up. If we say 'open marriage,' then if people find out either of us is doing something they would know it wasn't 'cheating.'"

I resolved to try to embrace an open marriage, to see what I might learn. I told Paul that of course I wanted joy and connection for him too. He'd been struggling, and if he thought it would help for him to be with other people, then I wanted that for him.

"As I give you permission, I'll add that if you go wild right now, I think it will hurt us," I said. "If you act in a way that seems unkind, then I might think less of you. I don't particularly want to share you with random people online. It's hard for me to imagine that being meaningful or good for you. But I know that you've made space for me to do what I've done, and so I will learn to handle the discomfort."

He met a French woman at a bar and they stayed out late talking. He made plans to see her when he was in Paris the following month.

Was this okay? Was that? I understood that negotiating boundaries, constantly discussing everything, was the price to pay for a nontraditional relationship. But sometimes it felt like parenting a toddler, where they kept pushing and pushing for something, and you constantly had to set limits or permit treats. Or maybe it was like making out with someone at Antioch College in the 1990s: *May I touch you over your shirt? May I unhook your bra?*

Sometimes it all seemed fine. Other times nothing seemed fine at all.

"When we retire, what should we do?" Paul asked one day over dinner.

Don't you need a job first before you can call it retiring? I thought. But I said the truth: "I'd like to teach more. I'm looking forward to being a grandmother. And at some point I'd like to look into becoming a foster parent for babies. What about you?"

"I'd like to go to Sandals Jamaica," he said.

When you lose regard for a spouse, how do you get it back? Is it on them to be more regardable? Or is it up to you to try to see them more generously? Was I thinking too much about "the marriage" and not enough about him as a person? When I was unmoved by how upset he was, was that me being a monster or myself for the first time, or both? I couldn't put my finger on what had changed. Everything was just as it had always been, but somehow it had become untenable.

I thought about one of Veronica's daughters. She was the tiniest thing, and when she got worked up her voice went higher and higher and she got cuter and cuter. When she complained about something, it was very hard not to smile at this little whistling teapot of a child. I pitied her in her adorableness.

Paul was not like that. When he got angry, I liked him less, though nor did I like him when he became cheerful, because the reason for his giddiness was the prospect of joining dating apps. Enlivened by the idea of putting together a profile, he became more helpful around the house. When he woke up in the middle of the night, he didn't wake me up to argue; he read a book, or he went and slept on the couch.

I didn't even know how to describe to people who asked what was happening with David. I considered showing them the description of "intimate friendship" from *The Chinese Pleasure Book* and the definition of "limerence," and the way his hand fit on my hip like it was designed for exactly that purpose.

Even with all that had been said on the subject—hours and hours of talking, writing hundreds of thousands of words on this very question—when Paul asked me to describe my feelings for David, and to tell him what I wanted, I tried to speak but couldn't.

On the way home from dinner at a restaurant where we'd tried to talk about other things, to get along, Paul and I got in a screaming fight in an empty park by the water.

"This was supposed to be something we were doing together! Now you're in love with someone else and I have to just sit there and watch it happen?"

"You pushed me to be in an open marriage and I didn't want to! But I agreed to try it! Then you said I could sleep with this person and just not fall in love with him! And I tried! But I'm not built that way! You started this! You wanted this! I was happy! And now I'm miserable! Yes, I love someone else, and I miss him so much but I'm here with you trying to make this all work and reading fucking *Polysecure*! Anyone else wouldn't have come back to you after California! Sometimes I wish I hadn't!"

Enraged, Paul threw, in a surprisingly graceful arc, our paper bag of leftovers into the river. I watched the food sail through the night and into the water. He kicked a trash can so hard it rocked on its pedestal. I thought he might throw himself over the railing and into the swirling water below. If he did, I wasn't sure how hard I would try to stop him.

I sat there on a bench by the water and wept as he stormed around like a Tasmanian devil on a loop in a cage. When he was facing away from me and at a distance, I began to walk swiftly in the other direction, wild-eyed, sobbing. I was a block away when my phone rang.

"I'm sorry I lost my temper," he said.

"It's okay," I said. "But I don't want to see you again tonight."

I took a shower, put on pajamas, got into bed. I made up the couch so he could sleep there. Earlier in the night he'd said he was worried I hated him. I'd said no, of course not. And I meant it. But as I fell asleep I thought, *I didn't then, but now I do.*

TWENTY-FIVE

The Opposite of a Scare

The day after the fight, Paul and I made up. He said that jealousy was just part of an open marriage and something we had to push through. He said I could see David as much as I wanted to and do whatever I wanted as long as he could too, and as long as Paul and I kept making each other the priority.

And so David and I met up at a book conference. Every second I did not have to appear on panels, we spent in bed at the hotel. I cared about nothing else but being close to him. We made out and cried and read to each other and couldn't stop talking.

The last night, David said after sex, "*That* seems like how a life gets created."

"Why does that make me happy?" I said. "Maybe it's the idea of trapping you."

"Oh, I'm already trapped," he said as he drifted off to sleep. "I've been trapped for a long time."

The next morning, we woke up at dawn to be awake together for an hour before he had to catch a flight back to make it to campus in time to teach his class.

We sat in silence on the couch, and I looked past him at the lights on a factory as we decided, once again, that this was too powerful, and that if we didn't get it under control it would end my marriage. I thought of *Brief Encounter*, and how sad the woman is when she gives up the doctor she's fallen in love with to stay with her husband: "Nothing lasts really. Neither happiness nor despair. Not even life lasts very long. There'll come a time in the future when I shan't mind about this anymore, when I can look back and say quite peacefully and cheerfully how silly I was. No, no, I don't want that time to come ever. I want to remember every minute, always, always to the end of my days."

David's alarm went off again. He got up, got dressed, and started to pull his things together.

"I have to go now," he said, and as he said it he was staring me in the eye, walking toward me where I sat on the bed, and pulling off his belt.

"You have to go," I said, and as I said that I was wrapping my arms around him and pulling him onto the bed. After we made love again, I helped him pack quickly, and then he was gone. He texted me later to say that he'd made it to the gate just before they shut the doors. I dreaded going home, where in spite of the joy I had spending time with Nate I also faced mountains of work and endless chores and a husband who I suspected was on OKCupid.

A couple of weeks after the book conference trip, my breasts were oddly sore, and I felt a little nauseous in the morning. I'd had spotting a few days after the trip; I pored over online discussions of "implantation bleeding" as if they were a lost codex. The odds were slim: at my age, getting pregnant naturally had a 3-to-5 percent chance each month. Staying pregnant after that was fifty-fifty. Then the chance of a genetic abnormality was at least one in twenty . . . Still. It wasn't *impossible*.

"Let's hope you're not," Veronica said. "At your age it's too dangerous. I love your hypothetical miracle child, but I love you more."

Not me. I loved my fantasy baby more than anything or anyone else. What's the opposite of a pregnancy scare? A pregnancy thrill? The thought of having a child with David made me feel high. Maybe there was still time. How clear everything would become if that were the case. He and I would have to be together. No one would question it.

I thought of something a woman had once said casually at a dinner party during a discussion of orphans: "They're usually good-looking."

"What are you talking about?" I asked her.

"You never heard that? Right, so, kids who go to orphanages are often illegitimate, meaning a lot of them were born out of wedlock to two sexy people who couldn't keep their hands off each other."

I imagined lust giving David and me a shockingly beautiful child.

At dinner that week with my parents, who I hadn't seen for a while, I noticed that my father looked frail. He had red-purple bruises on his arms. I noticed a yellow seed pod in his hair. I plucked it out with the words, "Dad, I'm going to take a flower off your head." He nodded.

I chatted with them in a friendly way even as I was picturing myself holding a baby on my lap as we ate. I imagined the child sleeping next to me in a car seat and almost levitated.

While I fantasized, my mother complained that my father refused to wear his hearing aids. We talked about the projects I was working on, and I told them I'd become friends with an editor named Helen. My mother said she'd host a dinner for Helen the next time she was around. I said, "No, thanks, when she's here it will just be me and her. I'm not sharing."

They did not know that I was in love, or that I was avoiding my glass of wine to prevent hurting a hypothetical miracle child.

We were eating at a restaurant near a college golf course. Outside, the birds chattered, and carts rolled in carrying happy, sweaty men with polo-encased bellies hanging over their shorts, white athletic socks pulled halfway up their calves. When my father went outside to smoke, I watched him through the window as the sun set behind him and the grass glowed red.

My mother was saying something about how well I'd arranged my life.

"It's not so great right now, actually. My marriage is in rough shape."

"Oh, did Paul do something?"

"Not him," I said. "Well, he did before. But this time it was me. I did something. I fell in love with someone else."

She was quiet for a few seconds as she absorbed this information.

"Is it Helen?" she said.

"No, not Helen."

"Tom Hanks?"

The next day, as I set off for a walk, a little girl from down the street who I'd spoken to a couple of times saw me and took off running as though we'd been kept apart by evil forces. When she reached me in front of my place, I could see that her flouncy white dress was covered in little red hearts. She raised her arms.

"You want me to pick you up?" I asked her. I'd read somewhere that it's good to ask kids this so that they know they have agency over their own bodies.

She said yes.

I lifted her into my arms. She snuggled into my neck and stayed that way as I carried her around. Her mother caught up with her and we chatted while I carried her daughter around. My arms grew tired, so I asked her if she wanted to get down and play. She did, so I ran inside and came out with a space suit from Nate's old costume box, which she put on immediately, and a ball, which she started bouncing.

Was her running to me a sign? I wondered. *Am I three weeks pregnant and she's the only person who can tell? Is there a soul in the bardo who wants me to bring her into the world?*

I liked to think about the bardo, a place where souls wait in between death and birth for the right opening to be reborn, to jump back in like life's a game of Double

Dutch. I thought of a Zadie Smith essay I'd read: "Isn't it bad enough that the beloved, with whom you have experienced genuine joy, will eventually be lost to you? Why add to this nightmare the child, whose loss, if it ever happened, would mean nothing less than your total annihilation?" She quoted Julian Barnes: "It hurts just as much as it's worth."

There was something about walking around living with a 3 percent chance of pregnancy—miniscule and yet greater than the zero percent chance I'd had in the years of post-vasectomy monogamy—that changed the color of the sky.

A week late according to my tracker app, I looked up "early pregnancy symptoms." I possessed all of them, including the more out-there indicators, like bluer veins. Beneath my skin ran Crayola-aquamarine rivers. I read the "implantation bleeding" page twelve more times and an article in *The Guardian* about a woman who had a healthy baby at forty-eight.

The next day I got my period. I bled for two weeks straight.

TWENTY-SIX

Getting to Lima

aby fantasies aren't always about literal babies!"
Veronica said. "They can be about anything creative. You have a book coming out. Focus on that,
not on getting dangerously pregnant."

Publishing a new book should have been thrilling, and
I enjoyed some parts of it. At my book party I hugged my
ninety-year-old neighbors and carried around a friend's
baby. I saw people from every place I'd ever worked. And
yet all of it provided only a momentary distraction from
the drive to see David again as soon as possible.

When a young photographer came to take my picture
for a profile connected to the book, she kept calling out
instructions for how to pose: "Casual gal! Girl boss! Broken doll! Serious gal! Broken girl boss doll in corner!"

"Broken girl boss doll in corner?" I said, laughing.

"Broken girl boss doll in corner *with a secret!"* she said.

I marveled at the pictures when I saw them a couple of weeks later in a newspaper. I looked like I had a secret.

I'd always loved book tours, and I was more grateful than ever to have an excuse to travel. I bought stacks of books and mailed them home. I wore dresses and heels and got manicures in bright colors. At one bookstore in the Midwest a young woman who'd already read the book said, "The way you talked about writing made me feel permission to say what I wanted to say without waiting for someone else to tell me it was okay."

"Is there a question there?" the moderator said protectively.

"Yes," I said, "a good question: *What do we let ourselves have?"*

At every event I did, I felt fully present. If attendance was low I became King Henry on St. Crispin's Day: "We few, we happy few." I wanted everyone to feel glad they'd come, like they were in on a glorious experience that everyone else would be sorry to have missed. The important thing was not to be like the teacher at Nate's school who yelled—at the end of a holiday show her creative direction had turned into a three-hour slog—"I guess let's do the last number even though *there's no one here!*" We parents who'd stuck it out looked at one another, all of us feeling like fools for not slipping out with the others during the interminable candy cane tap dance.

Every day I seemed to have another meaningful exchange with a stranger. At one outdoor event at a farmers market I signed fifty books with the wrong date, but no one seemed to care. During that reading a funeral procession passed by us, complete with bagpipes. As I browsed a library's ground-floor bookshop I heard a man on his way to the front door say something unintelligible.

"Sorry, what was that?" a security guard asked him.

"I was talking to *God*," the guy said.

"Ah, okay," said the guard.

He looked around to see if anyone else had heard that and only I had. We smiled at each other. Yes, of course. How silly of the guard not to have known that God, not he, was being addressed.

I stared out the windows of planes, trains, and cars, listening to the playlists David and I had made together. I watched clouds, industrial parks, and water speed by, the sun rise and set.

On a flight to a tour stop where I'd finally see David after what felt like a very long time, I started crying. That was all I did anymore the second I was alone. I had become a weeping prophet, only with no prophecy. I kept crying as the crew prepared for takeoff. I stared out the window, hoping the man in my row wouldn't notice and ask what was wrong. I imagined saying, "I'm married but in love with someone else who I haven't seen in weeks. My father is sick. My son is leaving soon for college. The Van Morrison song 'Hungry for Your Love' just came on in my headphones. And once I start crying these days it's really hard to stop."

Then a woman behind me started crying loudly enough to get the stewardess's attention.

"What's wrong, honey?" the flight attendant said, leaning into her row.

I didn't hear the words, just the universal sounds of frustration and loss.

"Don't you worry," the stewardess said in a soothing voice. "We'll get you to Lima."

I inhaled my neighbor's consolation the same way a character in *Ooka the Wise*, a book I read Nate when he was little, absorbs the smells from a neighboring tea shop to vicariously flavor his plain rice. The tenderness wasn't meant for me, but I'd take it. I stopped crying.

My phone filled with reviews and people reaching out to invite me to parties. One night in Nashville out for dinner with a group of writers, we got drunk on wine and sang "Frank Mills" from *Hair* at full volume from start to finish. At any time before that, I'd have been afraid of making a spectacle of myself. But I no longer cared what people thought about my subpar singing voice or about my love life. My unconventional marriage just made space for this other man, and for whatever Paul had going on. Not much so far, from what I could tell, but he seemed to be working to change that.

One night when I was doing a talk in Texas he made plans to have dinner with—*And really*, I thought, *of all the women on earth?*—Sarah, his not-just-emotional affair partner. After the event, I went out with a friend. I resolved to be fully present and not to check my phone to see what was happening back home.

I gave my dinner companion a rough sketch of what was going on.

"Oh! That's so hard!" she said with a clucking, maternal sympathy I found deeply lovable. "When I fell in love with my husband, I was so relieved I didn't ever have to do that again." She made the gesture of a lid clapping down on a jar.

"I love that you are content!" I said, trying to sound the way I felt, which was impressed, and not the way I could tell it came off, which was condescending. "I used to be like that."

She smiled, and said, "I hope it's okay if I tell you this: as you're talking about your husband I keep hearing you protecting him. And honestly, you're not being 'good' right now; you're being self-sacrificing, which is the opposite of real goodness. Part of me is rooting for you to surrender not only to love but also to the chaos of love. I want you to be selfish, to think about your own needs, to embrace getting what you want.

"And what interests me is that what you're talking about isn't having sex with multiple people, which anyone could do," she said. "Or having a secret emotional or sexual affair, which so many people do with various outcomes. What you're doing is honestly loving more than one person for an extended period of time, which is actually really unusual. I'll be curious to see how you pull it off. It seems fragile."

"Yes, it could blow up at any moment," I said.

"Yes," she said. "But so could anything."

TWENTY-SEVEN

Ghosts Behind Bars

As soon as I got back, Paul and I began going to couples therapy. He'd insisted on a therapist who specialized in polyamory, and I'd said fine. For the first forty minutes of the session the bespectacled older woman listened to our rundown. And then she spoke.

"It doesn't sound like you're in an open marriage," she said.

"What do you mean?" Paul said. "Of course we are."

"In an open marriage, a couple explores romantic or sexual relationships with other people as a way to enhance their own lives and their connection with each other," the therapist said. "They bring that energy back into the relationship, and it makes them a stronger couple. They have to negotiate boundaries and jealousy, and it's not for everyone, but it can work when there is commitment and communication. Is that what you have?"

I raised my hand. I knew the answer.

"No," I said.

"What I'm hearing in your case is that you, Paul, had at least one serious affair. You pushed your wife to embrace a nonmonogamous lifestyle that she didn't want. Because she missed exploring intimacy through kissing and she wanted to please you, she tried to go along with it. But because you had no clear containers or boundaries, and because you hadn't been honest about what you'd done or what you wanted, all hell broke loose. And now you're trying to make up for the regard you're not getting from your wife by seeking attention from other women."

"Young women!" I said, thrilled by how this was going.

"And *you*," she said, turning to me. I immediately regretted calling attention to myself. "Why did you put up with so many years of not kissing when that was a form of connection that mattered to you? You were setting yourself up for an explosion like this. And if you really didn't want his conception of an open marriage, why did you go along with it? Why didn't you stand up for yourself? And you should have known what was happening the second your feelings began for this other man. Why did you allow this relationship to unfold for so long, letting it reach this crisis point?"

It took me a second to realize that this last question wasn't rhetorical.

"Because I was scared by how strong my feelings were?"

"So you see now, don't you," the therapist said, like some kind of Lieutenant Columbo, LCSW, "that these are not the motivations of a couple lovingly exploring the world side by side? You're smart people. How is it you couldn't see that desire is unruly? Give it an inch and it will take a mile. Let it do what it wants, and it will brush away a lifetime's worth of care, self-denial, and strategy like a stray cobweb. Using words like 'polyamory' or 'primary versus secondary partners' keeps deep sexual and romantic attachments in check about as effectively as prison bars trap a ghost."

Was it appropriate to tip therapists? I wondered. *When they gave you really exceptional service? If they used ghost and prison analogies?*

We admitted that we did see that now, yes, and we slunk out of her office like kids who'd been caught setting off stink bombs in the school hallway. United in chagrin, we started getting along better.

In our next session, the therapist had us practice saying to each other, with detailed examples of why: "I'm sorry. Please forgive me. I love you. Thank you." We made lists of things we wanted to let go of and keep in our relationship.

I thanked him for all we'd been to each other over the years. I said that whatever else happened he could continue to put me down as his emergency contact. I would always have his back. I forgave him for his affair and for everything else and said that in one way or another we'd always be in each other's life because of Nate and also because we'd shared so much for so long. I said that more than we assumed was almost always possible, and that we could be creative as we figured out who we would be to each other going forward.

Paul apologized for having tried to push polyamory: "Maybe loving two men so much and sleeping with them when the two men represent such different things to you is literally impossible. It's a lot to hope for that if you're with two men you won't compare them, not drift away from one." He suggested that if I would give up David he would give up dating too. We could grow old together.

After the session, Paul went out for a run in the park, and I cleaned the kitchen while talking on the phone to Veronica. She said I needed to think about what I wanted and did Paul play any part in my future: "Now is not the time for him to be asking you to sacrifice anything. If I was his friend I'd point out to him that when his wife began grappling with a profound experience with another man, that was an existential crisis.

"I'd tell him to fight for her. And fighting for her in his case would look like getting a real job, helping more at home, not telling her to stop talking to anyone—and *definitely* not going on a dating app or chatting with someone he cheated with before. Maybe she still leaves, but at least he will make it harder for her to walk out, and he will know that he tried everything to keep her."

In a book of nineteenth-century sermons I'd found at a used bookstore, preacher Phillips Brooks says, "Shall not man bring his nature out into the fullest illumination, and surprise himself by the things that he might do?"

Who brought out my nature's fullest illumination? Clearly David. But was there something about my connection to Paul that also made me better, that I should preserve? I felt I owed it to him and to myself to take that question seriously.

When Paul got home from his run, I was saved from having to talk more about our therapy session by a phone call from an editor. I logged on to my laptop and saw that my inbox was full of urgent emails. Soon I was deep into Track Changes on a manuscript. Paul started doing Duolingo on the couch to prepare for his upcoming trip to France.

"*Non, monsieur!*" he said. *Ding!* "*Je suis anglais!*" *Ding!*

I put on headphones, but I could still hear him. I was working to support us. I was trying to stop being in love with someone else, or at least to let Paul date so he could feel better about it. I started sobbing.

"What's wrong?" Paul said. "I love you!"

I didn't reply. I didn't know what to say.

TWENTY-EIGHT

Running Slowly

I missed David so much that I began identifying with historical figures like Thecla, the first-century Turkish saint. After refusing to marry, she was stripped naked in the square and thrown onto a pyre to teach other girls not to second-guess their destinies. But before she was burned alive a storm came to put out the flames. I just wasn't quite sure what in my life was the fire and what was the rain.

I started paying close attention to people I met who'd radically changed their lives. Based on little indicators like how much they drank or how easily they smiled I tried to judge how happy they were. At a party at the home of someone who had fallen in love and left his wife,

I spotted one of his children eating tacos at the kitchen island. I guess it must have been hell for a while but then eventually there was his new wife talking about wallpaper and him getting ice for everyone's drinks.

I began to have an almost erotic fantasy of being settled enough that David and I could get into bed together at the end of a long day, watch an episode of *Law & Order*, kiss each other goodnight, and fall asleep. No weeping. No seven-hour conversations. Just a passive appreciation for Olivia Benson and holding each other while we slept.

Sometimes David would nobly say that he wanted to help me protect my family; that if he was the cause of us breaking up he worried I'd resent him. Other times he'd float less stoic options: "We could run off together *slowly*?"

Whatever we had gotten into, it certainly had not been fast. This was not the final scene in *The Graduate* where they look at each other in shock at the back of the bus.

I still refused to believe that's what was happening. And yet when you give birth you can't put the baby back inside you. David and I had love between us; there was no returning it to wherever it came from. The philosopher Ortega y Gasset said, "In loving we abandon the tranquility and permanence within ourselves, and virtually migrate toward the object." He said there's a remarkable similarity between mysticism and love—both he called forms of enchantment.

Still, I'd heard so many sad stories about divorce and its aftermath. My eleventh-grade English teacher was beautiful, with long red hair. She'd dressed up as Hester Prynne when talking about *The Scarlet Letter* and as Athena for teaching Greek myths. She talked to her women's literature students like we were her peers, which in retrospect was inappropriate but felt like respect at the time. She mentioned that when her husband left her, she thought people were whispering about her: "Maybe she wasn't good in bed."

Another time during a conversation about body image she pointed to her clingy maroon turtleneck dress and said, "You know what? I looked at myself in the mirror earlier and I said, 'Ms. Davis, that dress is so snug everyone can see the outline of your nipples!' Then I thought, *Why should I be ashamed? Women have nipples!*"

A few years after I graduated I came across an article about her. Since I'd lost track, she'd moved to California and started teaching there. One day she'd left her school keys behind with a farewell note on her classroom's blackboard, went to a body of water, and drowned herself, like Virginia Woolf. According to a news article I'd found, she'd left behind a teenage son.

There is an online community of women called What Would Virginia Woolf Do? It provides valuable information about hormones and navigating workplaces, but every time I see that name I think, *We know what she'd do. She'd fill her pockets with rocks and walk into the river Ouse.*

By her words and her example, my mother had instilled in me the virtue of holding on, of sticking it out, of remaining steadfast. Other people had tried to tell me that a divorce isn't necessarily a failed marriage, that successful marriages can successfully conclude. Thinking of my mother and my grandmother, I argued with such people. By definition, a marriage—a promise to stay joined until death—is a failure if it ceases before you die. Which aspect of "'til death do us part" did these people not understand?

Then one day my mother came over to pick up something, and I asked if I could talk to her. I told her how bad things were, and how I was in love with neither Helen nor Tom Hanks but a man named David, and I asked her what I should do. I said I'd taken to heart her advice that every time you leave one relationship and go into another you don't have fewer problems—just different ones, and so I'd done my best to live by her mantra, "The way you stay married is you don't get divorced." But now I was struggling.

I waited for her to tell me I should stay and tough it out. She paused before speaking and then she said, "What I should have said, was 'You don't get divorced—until you have to.'"

"What?" I couldn't quite believe what I was hearing. With a wave of her hand she'd just overturned one of the main edicts by which I'd lived.

"When I was the age you are now and having a hard time in my marriage, I wasn't in love with someone else. I don't know if that would have changed things. It might have. I'm happy to see you asking for more out of your life. You might live many more years. You deserve more than you've been letting yourself have."

I thought about my mother's desire for me to have more. She didn't have regrets, and said she'd had a wonderful life. But she also thought I was right to question staying.

I showed her a photo of David and me together.

"Oh! I *get* it," she said, zooming in on him.

As though she'd seen something in the photo, as with one of those Magic Eye pictures where the hidden image suddenly reveals itself, she said, while looking at my phone, "He loves you so much."

I burst into tears.

You can't guarantee that good things will happen to you, but you can make it so that if they do people won't say you don't deserve them. My mother's and grandmother's lives seemed more relevant to the discussion of what to do now than any academic questions about sexual ethics. I wanted to see what it could be like now to let love and creativity be more of a priority than obligation or responsibility.

The next time I saw David we again spent most of the day in bed. These out-of-time hours with him felt like, as author Akhil Sharma said of the days he spent falling in love with his wife, a picnic without ants.

One night, I began drowsing with my head on his chest, listening to his heartbeat, when I thought I heard his heart stopping. In that moment of imagined death, scenes from a shared life flashed before my eyes, only it was a life we hadn't lived yet. We'd fallen asleep and woken up together for thousands of nights. We'd fought and made up. We'd walked through cities all over the world in every kind of weather. We'd hosted dinners with our friends. We were grandparents together. And now it was over. He was gone! Tears started running down my face.

"Why are you crying?" he said, suddenly wide awake. "What's wrong?"

"Nothing," I said. "It's dumb. I imagined you dead and I was sad. Don't die first. I couldn't take it."

"Me either," he said. "We should try to die at the same time."

"Or let's not die at all?"

TWENTY-NINE

Pride and Grammar

Emerson said all days are Judgment Day. We are faced with endless choices about how to be. Paul and I decided to be as civilized and kind as possible and to keep things as normal as we could for Nate, who fortunately was enough in his own world not to be paying too much attention to us.

When I went back on tour, Paul hung out again—and then a third time—with Sarah.

It seemed possible that she would become his girlfriend. I felt that I was in no place to argue. I partly wished for it, imagined that then things would become clearer. Paul dropped Nate at a study-abroad program in France and spent a few days there on his own. Noticing that he'd charged champagne to his room, I frowned at my banking app.

I'd taken advantage of my time alone to schedule freelance gigs and readings. As I drove from one city to another, I called Paul. I talked to him through the car's speakers as he walked through the streets of Paris, stopping occasionally for a glass of wine or an espresso. He said he was trying to go out that night and was disappointed that the French woman he'd met at the bar was out of town.

"Have you been in touch with Sarah?" I asked.

"We've been texting some," he said.

I listened. I asked questions. I stayed calm. I did not say anything to suggest that I was upset. I said I'd have to do the *Polysecure* work to find a way to handle the feelings that stirred up, that he was or soon would be sleeping with that woman. Well, sleeping with her again. He'd made space for me to have a relationship with David and I needed to make space for him to have an intimate friendship too.

After we hung up, I began lecturing myself: All human beings are polyamorous because we all love various people in different ways. We shouldn't look at any of this as coming out of deficits: "I can't get what I want here. I'll get it there." We should look at each person as a fellow human being who we . . .

My thoughts trailed off and were replaced by a blazing rage. I drove for a few more miles and then I screamed in the car, "What the fuck am I doing?"

Why was I trying so hard to be okay with something I hated? Why was I working to make the money, even affording Paul a European jaunt? Why was I keeping a man on the side who made me more myself and with whom I'd had *a mystical experience*?

I thought of a line from Marilynne Robinson's *Gilead*: "And often enough, when we think we are protecting ourselves, we are struggling against our rescuer."

As I drove on through the late-afternoon rain and Paul fell asleep thousands of miles away having no idea how I felt, I ended our marriage in my heart.

A few days later, I flew to Europe to join Paul and Nate for a long-before-planned trip to Germany to see a religious production put on by the town of Oberammergau. When the Bavarian town survived the bubonic plague in 1633, they promised God that every ten years forevermore they would do a Passion Play telling the story of Jesus. On the Ash Wednesday before they do the play, the town issues "the Hair and Beard Decree," meaning that no one in the show can cut their hair until after the show wraps.

Having been raised without religion and regretting it,

I'd given Nate a baseline faith. He was free to reject it all, but at least he had something to push against. One of his godmothers had given him a graphic-novel version of the Bible, and he'd read it several times. In Oberammergau, we watched the five-hour show (with dinner break). There were dozens of people in the cast, from babies to old people, with a choir of about sixty. There were even camels and horses. The hammering of the nails into the actors' hands was so realistic I flinched. When Judas hanged himself, Nate leaned over and whispered, "That wasn't in *The Action Bible*."

The trip proved that Paul and I could still travel together, still be parents together, even though our marriage was over. We slept in the same room, but as at home, we did not touch. One night when Nate was out picking up a near-the-Berlin-Wall rock for his friend as a joke present Paul and I had a drink together. We were getting along well. The wine and the foreign city and the night got to me. I was feeling tender.

I didn't know what this new sense of well-being in his presence meant. Would we be closer now? This was the father of my child, and I'd felt like there was no intimacy left to us, but now I wasn't sure. It was the first time I'd felt anything like that about him in a long time. Had I been reckless in wanting to leave the marriage?

He said we should talk about what things were going to be like when we got back home.

"Yes, you go first," I said. I wondered if he was feeling the same way I was, if he would take my hand and look into my eyes, tell me that whatever I wanted I could have, that he was going to fight for me, wait for me, as long as it took. I wasn't sure that it would make a difference to the outcome. I had a feeling I would still make the choice to leave. But perhaps there would be a sweet denouement.

He took a sip of his drink. Then he said, "We keep getting closer on this whole me-and-other-people thing and not pulling the trigger. I'd like you to acknowledge that I'll be dating."

He saw my face fall.

"Why?" he said. "What were you going to say?"

Surely I didn't really think that I'd be able to find a third path between divorce and never speaking to David again ("If I'm attracted to my neighbor we move")? When I fell in love with someone else, what did we think was going to happen? Or was this the third path, leaving slowly?

What was clear was that Paul and I had thought we were somehow supremely enlightened. One of our downfalls was pride. La Rochefoucauld wrote: "There are two kinds of faithfulness in love: one is based on forever finding new things to love in the loved one; the other is based on our pride in being faithful." I'd taken real pride in having stayed married like my mother and grandmother. I felt there was nobility in sticking it out. But was that enough to build a life on—bragging rights?

Friends asked why we split up, and I didn't know what to say. Was it his cheating? Was it my falling in love? Was it the money problems? Was it a divergence in values? Was it the space between foster parenthood and Sandals Jamaica? Was it that all of this came to the fore in the same year? Why wasn't I able to name a single cause of death?

Maybe because he pushed me for a more open marriage, and the second I started to take the idea seriously I fell in love with someone else who made me feel like some more essential, truer version of myself that I was then unwilling to abandon. If that's the story, was it the pusher or the faller who deserves the blame?

Perhaps in our relationship it was Paul's role to be the one pushing for expansion, my job to contract. Once I started expanding too, the system stopped functioning. Maybe if he'd contracted at that point, then we'd have survived. Maybe I should have done that myself. No one will ever know. There are no control studies when it comes to a marriage.

A friend in graduate school once told me about her

grammar dissertation. She said one approach to grammar is proscriptive: "Thou shalt not split an infinitive." The other is descriptive, explaining what people do rather than what they *should* do—so, the way we all use "hopefully" to mean we hope it will work out when the word started out meaning something done *with* hope.

"Everyone wants a grammar to be complete, consistent, and determinative," she said. "That's not possible. There's a craving for determinism, but there's no such thing. The world is indeterminate and uncertain. Looking into the past we can construct a narrative to explain how we got from one place to the other. But if it was plausible, why wasn't it predictable?"

Plenty of marriages survive worse than what we did to ours. Why didn't ours survive when others did? A lack of willpower? Too many stresses on it in too short a time? Or had it just run its course? I wondered if we could see our marriage not as cut short but rather completed, a lifelong friendship or kinship entering a new phase. Do we say that because a person dies their life was unsuccessful? All things end one way or another. There are ways for both their duration and their ending to be graceful or miserable. I'd been happy in my marriage for a long time. But we had diverged, and I was not happy in it anymore.

In couples therapy Paul read me a letter he'd written acknowledging his mistakes and saying that he thought we should try again. He pointed out that it would be better for Nate if we stayed together. Images from *Afterschool Specials* about children's lives ruined by their parents' separating flashed before my eyes.

On a call with Veronica I asked her if she thought I was making a mistake getting a divorce. "Children, even fully grown ones, are conservative," she said. "He would surely want his parents together. But he's going to be out of the house soon. At some point you need to let this choice be about the rest of your life and not about what your child—who doesn't really know you as people out in the world, only as his parents—at this precise moment thinks is best."

I loved my son so much though. I didn't want him to be sad for a second. And now here I was about to make him sad. Even if he'd understand one day. Even if I'd have wanted my own mother to be true to herself if I'd been in his position.

"Part of being an adult is knowing how to take a loss," Veronica said. "And this is going to sound mean, but aside from Nate's feelings, which of course are not nothing, there's not so much to lose. Whatever man you wind up with or don't, you're going to have a love-filled life.

CRUSH

And you have a number of compelling reasons to break up. You're tired of the money problems and the open marriage pressure, and you learned that he was unfaithful and lied about it. By pushing you to be with other men he was guilty of a failure of imagination. He should have known you better. You're lionhearted. And now it's too late to do anything about it: you're madly in love with someone else.

"And whoever's fault it is, the falling in love is done now. You can't undo it. When you start out with a bunch of baking ingredients, you can wind up with a loaf of bread or croissants or a cake. But at some point in the process, that's not true anymore. It is what it's going to be. Once you're in that deep, there's no turning it into another kind of relationship. You can't un-bake a birthday cake. And honestly, why would you want to? You'd need a compelling reason to stay. You can still love Paul but not want him anymore."

She summarized her advice this way: "What is love asking your soul to do? Do that. Then imagine the most beautiful future you can. Point yourself in that direction. And *go*."

That night I went to a party thrown by a friend in the country. Her long-divorced parents were there, both of them with their new partners, the father cooking food

213

for everyone, the mother telling stories, kids running around with dogs, old and new friends talking and laughing, everyone eating outside together as the sun set and the fireflies came out. I thought of the song "Crowded Table," and decided that might be a good goal.

If I was going to leave my marriage I wanted it to be because the marriage was over in and of itself and not because I'd found someone else I preferred. And so I'd never told David how seriously I was considering getting a divorce until I was sure. Then one day on the phone I did.

"I want you," I said.

"What do you mean?" he said.

"I want to sleep with you every night. I want to comfort you when you're sad. If I win an award I want you to be my date to the ceremony. I want us to go to our parents' funerals together. I want to catch your colds. Do you want that?"

"Pay the fuck attention!" he said. "Of course I do."

THIRTY

New Old Home

Running toward love is not easy for grown-ups with full lives. I didn't want to pull Nate out of his final months of high school and move him to another state. David didn't want to abandon his tenured job and move in with me, jobless and dependent. We decided we would stay long distance for a while.

This would allow us to consider exactly how we wanted to construct our new life. Was seeing our names together on a mortgage or marriage license necessarily the ultimate fulfillment of what we had? Was the revelation I'd received nothing more than that I should become a wife again, this time as a faculty spouse? If we were going to treat love as a verb and not as a noun, what would that entail?

My parents had recently moved out of my childhood home, and so Nate and I took it over. Except for the days he was at his father's, he slept in what had been my old bedroom. I slept in what had been my parents'. The walls were in the same place but the furniture was new, cobbled together from various basements and websites. The return gave me an uncanny feeling, as though it were several different eras at once, and I was various ages.

Strolling through the neighborhood, I was cast back to times I walked around to get out of the house when I was a teenager. I remembered different incarnations of myself and my parents, the kinds of things we ate, how we'd all been dressed. I saw, out of the corner of my eye, my childhood pet rabbit hopping around, gnawing on baseboards.

Unused to having so much space, I felt like a cat hiding under a couch. My father's former office I left empty. I worked at the kitchen table until finally one day I got up the courage to buy a desk and put it in the room that had once been his. It took weeks but eventually I was able to work in there without feeling like I was going to get in trouble.

I found a stack of old photos. One showed me at age seven with my mom smoking in the kitchen—where I now made breakfast for Nate. Another was of my father smoking next to his dictionary, in which I looked up words as a little girl, in the office where I now tried to make a living. When I was sixteen, a burglar had come in over an air conditioner and I'd scared him off coming home from my job at one in the morning. That window was right there by my head as I slept. When I heard a noise in the middle of the night, I checked the locks.

I tried to make the place my own, to create new and happy memories there. I returned from walks with flowers to set out on the table, new lamps for the living room, and food to make for Nate. I felt more like myself living on my own, even if I was technically still married.

Paul and I stayed in therapy to try to figure out how to split up in a way that would be easiest on us and on Nate. For the Zoom session we appeared on the screen in separate squares because we were each in our own apartments. When he waved his hands to make a gesture, I noticed something.

"Are you not wearing your ring?" I said.

"Oh, I've been taking it off for dates," he said. "I forgot to put it back on."

"I was leaving mine on because I assumed we'd have a conversation about it before we did."

"This is a *moment*," our therapist said.

"No, I'm actually relieved," I said. "I thought it was going to be a hard conversation when I asked if you were okay with me taking mine off. Now we don't have to talk about it." I pulled my ring off and held up my hand. The jewelry that had been put on my finger in a ritual before witnesses, then stayed there for so many years, now had been taken off without ceremony, and with only Paul and the therapist there to see it happen.

"How's Paul going to support himself?" Veronica asked me the next time I talked to her.

"He'll take half of whatever we have now and then I think he will figure it out," I said.

My mantra when asked about the reasons for the divorce was: "There are no bad guys here." Though my lurking fear was that if you were saying that, it was likely that *you* were the bad guy. For whatever it was that Paul did wrong, the fact was, I was the one who left.

Paul came over for family dinners every Sunday and I liked him much more once we were separated. Once we were no longer romantic partners I was able to love him as Nate's father and as a member of my family. In so many ways, we'd raised each other. He got a full-time office job he loved and a sweet, pretty girlfriend. Interestingly, it was not Sarah. That had fizzled out quickly.

But it was someone he adored and who adored him. They took Nate and his friends to basketball games. With her, Paul became a more grounded and happier version of himself. If he'd been holding me back, I'd clearly been doing the same for him.

THIRTY-ONE

Look to the Weasel

When I went to pick up uncontested divorce paperwork at the county clerk's office, I wandered the courthouse looking for the room number I'd written on a sticky note. I was lucky to find the place just a few minutes before they took an hourlong lunch break. The somber, bespectacled civil servant in a navy sweater over a tie and button-down handed me the documents. Behind him an unseen woman sang along with Diana Ross on the radio. The "Contested Matrimonials" clerk sat by the window like a child in time out.

"Okay, so this page is the form you'll need to get to the defendant," my clerk said. "Are you in touch?"

"Perhaps more than is strictly necessary," I said, and he laughed.

As I went off to fill out the documents, I felt like I'd been let into a secret club, one with mechanical stampers and drugstore notaries who for two dollars will sign their name and affix a seal on your separation agreement.

The next day, after getting the pages notarized, I was about to go through the court's metal detector to drop them off when I remembered: "The postcard!" I said. "I forgot the postcard!" You were supposed to include a stamped postcard so the court could let you know when you were officially divorced.

I walked back out of the court and down the block to a shop and paid $1.50 for a postcard. Then I looked up the closest post office to buy a stamp. It was the Federal Plaza building. I had to go through a big lobby with an "FBI Heroes" scrolling display and signs about immigration and naturalization services. At the post office a young blond guy was complaining to the postal lady about his boss. He needed *plain* stamps for a mailing. He was going to have to send a photo of the stamps to his boss before buying them.

"They're flags," she said. "It's the most basic stamp there is."

"You don't know my boss," he said. "One time I got chewed out for getting Yogi Berra stamps."

"Well," she said, "maybe he was a Red Sox fan! If a stamp was a team that wasn't mine I'd throw it back in your face! What about a classic stamp, though? *Peanuts*?"

The young man shook his head sadly.

When it was my turn, I asked for Lunar New Year stamps, but they were out. "Okay," I said, "I'll take anything but the 'Love' ones." The 'Love' stamp showed a simpering cat holding a giant heart.

"You don't like cats?" she said. "I don't love cats either."

"No, I like cats. I'd just prefer something less sappy. This is going on a divorce postcard."

She nodded, riffled through her cache, and handed me a sheet of "Mighty Mississippi" stamps.

"Exactly right," I said, and gave her seven dollars.

Back at the courthouse, I gave the clerk my forms. He looked them over and stamped them in big block letters: UNCONTESTED.

"Where'd you get this postcard?" he said.

"Down the street."

"You know what this is?"

"The Polo Grounds."

"I figured you'd be too young to know that."

"Yeah, I'm pretty old."

Then I took the papers to a room on the first floor where I found myself alone with two solemn, impeccably dressed women behind the counter. A quiet room. It looked a lot like my elementary school's main office with big wire baskets and paper labels, light streaming through the windows. One of the women was watching a political speech from a decade earlier as if it were a breaking news report, but she looked up to say, in a tone of voice that was neither cheerful nor ominous, "Good luck."

Moving was expensive, but start to finish the divorce itself cost just $325, plus the cost of the postcard. Paul and I were still cordial. And yet, I struggled to metabolize the present; there was no way to step back and consider either the past or the future. When Veronica's younger daughter played Roses and Thorns, the how-was-your-day game Paul and I used to play with Nate each night at dinner, she picked things that had happened nanoseconds before. Veronica would say, "What about earlier today? At school? Or at softball?" And still she would say, "Nope. My rose was being served these mashed potatoes."

Veronica said, "That's what it's like when you make decisions when you're in a heightened state of emotion. You only see that instant, not the whole picture. Try to take in each new piece of information you receive now.

See if it's useful in helping you determine how you want to spend your afternoon or the rest of your life."

While Paul and I were friendly, it was still odd when Nate and I went over to Paul's place, which used to be our place. I saw the plants I'd planted in the pots, the sisal twine I'd wound around the pipes to keep the baby from burning himself when he started crawling, the dishes I'd bought at Ikea. When Paul and his girlfriend hosted gatherings together there, she served food out of pots we'd received as wedding presents with serving spoons I'd used for toddler Nate's mac and cheese. It was like being shown around by a *Christmas Carol* ghost, being made aware of what changed and what didn't without me around, and of all the ways that I was no longer the same person I'd been when I lived there.

I left one of their parties early to go home and watch the BBC adaptation of *Pride and Prejudice*. I'd remembered very little of it from when I saw it in the 1990s except Colin Firth in the wet undershirt. But this time around, watching it alone in bed, I was struck by the moment when Elizabeth Bennett finds Darcy completely changed and says, "I can't imagine what's caused him to become so altered." Her aunt says, "Can't you?"

There is a kind of trauma high, a pink cloud that follows something very terrible or very wonderful, and I was in it. I kept walking in the wrong direction, and I kept falling down. My blood seemed to want to escape my body. Blood seeping out from the finger I cut slicing oranges and crusting on my knee where I'd nicked it on a table corner in the dark. For so long I'd enjoyed thinking of myself as a responsible person, an excellent citizen. And now I could no longer check "married" on official forms; my credit score was down a hundred points; my kid was forever a child of divorce; I was covered in blood; and my phone screen had a thousand cracks.

For the first time in my life, a life spent driving just three miles over the speed limit, I was pulled over by the police.

"Do you know why I stopped you?" the cop asked as I handed him my license and registration.

"No, but I'm sorry, whatever it is," I said.

"You have a taillight out."

"Oh, I didn't know. I'll get it fixed."

"It's okay. No reason to cry about it."

"Am I crying?" I reached up to my face and found that my cheeks were wet. "Sorry, it's a weird time."

He handed me a fix-it ticket. "Get that light replaced and you're all set. Maybe sit for a minute and calm down before you pull back out. Drive safe."

"Thank you, officer," I said.

"I got a ticket," I said the next time I spoke to Veronica. "I keep falling down. I'm a mess."

"No, you're just more whole now," Veronica said. "Take some time off if you can. Realize that even if you're not working all the time you deserve to live. And go see David again already."

He and I met up in Florida. One morning we drove to the ocean at dawn. He read to me while we waded in the water and smiled at the dogwalkers. On our way back to the car I tripped in the empty parking lot. As I was falling, I saw his face turn to me, panicked. He spiked the water bottle he was carrying and reached out. He pulled me back up and dusted me off and looked me over and asked a thousand times if I was okay.

As we kept walking, I assured him that yes, I was fine. And that he'd been very sweet. I told him that I'd fallen on a sidewalk next to Paul when we were fighting. He'd been afraid I was going to yell at him for tripping me—and so he'd yelled at me before he checked to see if I was hurt. The spiked water bottle was healing.

"Well, it would have been more reparative if I'd kept you from falling down in the first place," David said.

But how could I ever regret how anything had gone, even the less than perfect parts, when all of it had brought me to this place—my skinned knee stinging but David leaning over from the driver's seat, his hair salty and damp from the ocean, his hand gently pulling the strap of my bathing suit off my shoulder?

In *The Angel That Troubled the Waters*, Thornton Wilder wrote: "Without your wound where would your power be? It is your very remorse that makes your low voice tremble into the hearts of men. The very angels themselves cannot persuade the wretched and blundering children on earth as can one human being broken on the wheels of living. In Love's service only the wounded soldiers can serve."

I made new friends. At a party for a young writer whose book I'd blurbed I fell into conversation with two men. I asked how they knew each other. One was an old friend of the host. The other was his boyfriend. They'd met a few months earlier online. When the boyfriend left to mingle, I said, "You two seem very in love."

"We are," the man said and sighed. "And I'm a little old to be falling this in love for the first time. Being in love is the best thing that's ever happened to me and the hardest. I've come to realize that so many things I thought were important just aren't. I've had to rethink everything I thought I knew."

"They don't tell you how being in love is hardest when

you really care," I said. "Well, I guess they did in *Moon-struck*."

"Do you love him, Loretta?" my new best friend said, quoting Olympia Dukakis.

"Aw, ma, I love him awful," I said, quoting Cher.

Together, both of us quoted Olympia Dukakis: "Oh, that's too bad."

"Remember how they go to the opera?" he said. "When I dreamed of having a partner, I imagined us going to plays and the ballet. For the rest of our lives we'd be doddering around theaters, holding hands. But on our first date, I took him to a play. In retrospect, it wasn't the best introduction for him, but I love Beckett. Through all of *Endgame,* he sighed loudly. So loudly that people were turning around. I've asked him since if he wanted to go to things and he's said no."

"I know we just met," I said, "but I'll go to the theater with you."

"I might take you up on that," he said.

David and I resumed our perpetual book club. We read Annie Dillard together, and we both circled what she said about weasels: "The thing is to stalk your calling. . . . I think it would be well, and proper, and obedient, and pure, to grasp your one necessity and not let it go, to dangle from it limp wherever it takes you."

Since David and I had started talking, I'd had more new experiences than at any time since babyhood, when I was learning to walk and talk and eat solid food. Loving him had been my liberation. Everything had blown up and everything seemed deliriously possible.

THIRTY-TWO

The Layton Prize

From what would become his deathbed, my father complained about an award he had won that he didn't want, the Layton Prize. It came with money and a trophy, but he said he'd rather not have his name associated with it. I searched through his email to learn more. I looked online. I checked every spelling of the name. Eventually, I realized: there was no Layton Prize.

He became increasingly tormented by the thought of this award. He couldn't get comfortable, agonizing about the Layton Prize.

"Dad, would you like me to decline the Layton Prize on your behalf?" I asked him.

"Oh! That would be great," he said.

"My pleasure. Would you like me to say, 'We politely

decline the Layton Prize'? Or 'We respectfully decline the Layton Prize'?"

"Respectfully."

"Done."

Then he was able to settle down and sleep.

As we die, our minds go all sorts of places. We can't hold it against a person, what they think about in those final days. My father's mind, circling the drain of consciousness— he called it "a surrealist repertory theater"—preoccupied itself not with thoughts of his soon-to-be-widowed wife, or his divorcing daughter, or his college-bound grandson, but rather with an unworthy, imaginary accolade. He monologued, too, about his parents having disappointed him. His mother had died at 102. He said his father had sucked all the air out of the room; everything revolved around him.

"I have no idea what that must be like," I said.

Even in the throes of near-death he clocked the sarcasm.

"Yeah, you got some of that," he said, "but you didn't have it as bad."

He wanted me to read to him. I went and got a stack of books off the shelf the same way I did when Nate was little. I read a page or two from each. He shook off everything from P. G. Wodehouse to Shakespeare, saying all of it was "too thinky."

Of my impending divorce he said only, "I knew the marriage wouldn't work out."

"Okay," I said, and fed him mashed-up strawberries.

At around three in the morning he said he didn't like how he felt and wondered if there might be a quicker way. It took me a minute to realize he was asking me to kill him.

"I'm not going to do that," I said. "I'm sorry, but I think the only way out of this is through."

He rolled his eyes and muttered something about New Age bullshit.

"How long will it take?" he said.

"As long as you need," I said. "No longer and no shorter. Everyone has to go through it. Most people throughout history have suffered and had no one to help them. But you won't be in pain, and you won't be alone."

From memory, he recited a bit of a William Blake poem, "Oh Jerusalem!"

Bring me my bow of burning fire!
Bring me my arrows of desire!

I looked it up on my phone and read the rest of it to him.

From memory I recited Yeats's "The Four Ages of Man."

Together we did the first page of T. S. Eliot's "The Love Song of J. Alfred Prufrock."

Looking on, my mother clapped. I was glad we'd made her happy. Even under the circumstances, she remained stylish and feisty, showing up for each day in black jeans and full makeup no matter how bleak the agenda.

"Auden: 'If equal affection cannot be, let the more loving one be me,'" I said.

"Auden didn't say that," my father said, bringing the volley to an end.

"What do you mean he didn't say it?" I said. "Of course he said it. It's from his poem 'The More Loving One.' It's on the plaque outside his building."

"Allen Ginsberg made it up."

"Hmm," I said. I decided to let it go. "Well, doesn't it seem like something he *would* have said? Do you remember what he wrote back when Christopher Isherwood asked him to marry Erika Mann to get her a British passport and save her?"

"No."

"One word: 'DELIGHTED.' Isn't that *great*? Whenever I get asked to do anything—blurb a book, moderate a talk, watch a friend's baby, if I say yes I try to say it like that—'Yes, I'd be *delighted*.' I think about Auden, about being the more loving one, and so I never resent doing favors. Because isn't it a gift, being given the opportunity to do a good deed? Aren't we lucky to be asked?"

"Hmm," he said, and went back to sleep.

I felt lucky to be there with him, to keep him as comfortable as possible with the help of the "comfort pack" of medications I'd picked up from the hospital pharmacy. At first, he hadn't wanted to accept the help of hospice, even though the nurse visits and equipment and medications were free and offered us support in caring for him. Only once I began referring to hospice as "drug concierge" was he persuaded of its value. The administrator did an intake, gave us an oxygen tank, a walker, and moral support, then left a phone number to call if we needed anything.

Every few hours, at his request, I helped him from his bedroom to the living room, then back again. I held him around his chest as he stagger-glided across the floor leaning on his walker. I felt his heart beating against his ribs like a bird knocking against the walls of a cage.

The last time he asked me to take him, it was harder for him to walk. Together my mother, Aunt Kath, and I wrangled him back into the bed and nestled him under the comforter. It was so much like putting a child to bed. I put some classical music on my phone, which I set on the nightstand. He closed his eyes.

My mother, aunt, and I went and sat in the living room. A few minutes later I went back to check on my father and my phone. I walked into the room. Beethoven's Violin Concerto in D Major was playing. My father's eyes were open, and he was gazing out the window, through which afternoon light was streaming. He looked happier than he had in a long time. I stood there looking at him for a minute, and then for another minute. He hadn't blinked. I reached over to my phone and turned the music off.

"Dad?" I said.

I put my hand on his arm. He didn't move. I couldn't tell if he was still breathing. I stared. It seemed at first as if he was, but I couldn't tell if it was a trick of the light. His heart, so furious against my hand a few minutes earlier, was still.

My father and Beethoven and I had been in that room and now it was just me. I absorbed this new reality and then went into the living room.

"Kath?" I said, asking her if she'd come in. She and my mother both did. Kath gently pulled back the covers and checked his pulse.

"He's gone," she said. "He waited for us to be out of the room. I've heard that a lot of people do that. They want to be alone."

My mother and Kath and I stood there.

"He looks so young, doesn't he?" my mother said, staring

at his face, which had lost all its tension. "He looks like he did when I met him."

My mother usually waited for five p.m. sharp to have a cocktail, but on that day she mixed us vodka cranberries at three.

Each of us, my mother in particular, had been consumed by his needs and his will and his presence for a long time. Now he needed nothing else, except for us to contact the saintly hospice nurse one last time, which I did, and to take calls or to decline calls and then to discuss what to do about all the calls. Then to say goodbye as the funeral home director came over and bundled him into a red velvet bag that looked remarkably like the sleep sack Nate slept in as a baby.

"Look how cozy!" my mother said, relieved that they were not using a zippered plastic body bag. We watched as he was carried out, looking thirty years old instead of eighty. As he crossed the threshold of the house, I whispered, "Goodbye, Dad." My eyes spontaneously filled with tears like water seeping out of the ground.

When David got off calls with the older members of his family, they'd say, "Very good . . . Very nice . . . So, that's it," on repeat with various intonations until someone hung up. He and his sister did that with each other as a joke: "So, that's it!" "So . . . that's it?" "*So*, that's it."

There would be no more conversations with my father. We'd had our last fight, shared our last meal. The men from the funeral home slid my father's body into their hearse. My arms ached from having hoisted him into his bed the last time. *So*, I thought, as I watched the men drive him away from the house and up the driveway, *that's it*.

THIRTY-THREE

An Education

During the final weeks of my father's life David and I talked throughout each day. Most nights we also sent each other—and I don't know how this started, only that it was the best thing I'd ever seen on a screen, better than *Clueless*, better than *The Wire*—short instructional videos we made each other, presented in a community college lecture format.

There were lessons explaining the buttons on flannel shirts, the clasps of a bra. As a teacher, I was exasperated with the administration, which continued to refuse me a parking spot closer to campus, and with my hapless students, who stumbled over basic skills like unzipping a zipper: "Because this has been a recurring question in

CRUSH

office hours: No, you don't pull it up, you pull it *down*, like this."

He played the part of a fresh-out-of-a-master's-program sincere instructor who believed deeply in his students' potential, espousing lofty aphorisms about the power of education as he pulled off a blazer, exposing his muscular arms: "Did you know that a C minus can be the best thing that ever happened to you if you take it in the right spirit?"

We both showed up for class even when we were tired, because it was our job and because deep down we really did feel for those dumb kids who needed twenty lessons in how to take off a shirt.

The morning before my father died, David had Zoomed in, clothed, while I was making pancakes. I told him to talk to my mother and aunt for a minute while I got the last ones off the griddle. Then I grabbed my laptop and whisked him into the other room. When I returned, the two women were aflutter.

"He's *very* handsome!" Kath said. "He looks like a boarding-school headmaster who could also build you shelves."

"Yes, and you just like him immediately!" my mother said.

When I told him the Auden line that my father in his delirium had dismissed, he said, "I'd *always* prefer to be the lover than the beloved. The lover gets to *love*."

Again, so sweet. So sincere. He kept after me about considering Petrarch.

At the end of the day my father died, Nate arrived at what was now just my mother's house along with more members of the family. We sat around and ate and talked. While I refilled coffee cups and listened to everyone's stories, I realized that my relationship with my father hadn't changed very much over time, but by the time he died I had changed.

In college, my flirtatious astronomy professor had told me on the phone one night that NASA had sent a capsule into space, Voyager II, with messages in many languages, photos of human beings, and a map of our DNA, "basically everything they'd need to wipe us off the map." Sharing my inner thoughts and hopes with my father had often felt like this—handing him the tools to hurt my feelings. And again and again, he did.

He had a talent for uttering lapidary phrases that stuck in my head and took on the weight of scripture. Some were elegant and funny. Of a county fair demolition derby: "Your whole life you try not to run into other cars. And then for a few glorious moments that's the goal." Others were confusing. He'd say, of something I'd written that he didn't like, "It doesn't seem like you had fun writing it."

What does that mean? I'd wonder. *Am I having fun writing this?* I'd ask myself as I looked at my computer screen for years, for decades. If I asked him what he'd meant by a line like that he rarely remembered saying it. But what he said continued to matter to me even when it became clear that he'd just liked the sound of those particular words coming out of his mouth in that moment.

In Oceania, a Vanuatu tribe formed a cargo cult around Prince Philip in the middle of the last century, believing him to be the son of a mountain spirit. That was like me and my father. I never could stop hoping for his affection and approval. I was repeatedly popping up out of a Whac-A-Mole board like it was my job to get hit.

That ended the week he died. Where in the past I would have told him what I was thinking about, even knowing he'd probably say something that would hurt my feelings, I held back. Many times in those final days, I almost said, "I'm in love. He's wonderful. He's so smart and kind. You don't need to worry about me being alone."

But I didn't. Because the truth was he wasn't worried about me; he wasn't thinking about me at all. If my whole life I'd been Charlie Brown running to kick Lucy's football, now, for the first and last time, I was hugging Lucy and saying, "I love you, so I'm going to spare us this depressing charade."

At the last possible moment I learned that to be the more loving one to him I had to stop being vulnerable. I learned, at last, to pay the fuck attention, to love him for who he was, not to set him up to disappoint me and then blame him for doing exactly what we both knew he would do.

I stayed silent. I fed him berries. I tucked him into bed. I played him Beethoven. I felt his heart beating and then not beating. I buried him. That would have to do.

THIRTY-FOUR

The Lynd Wurm

Maybe I shouldn't have tried to go anywhere so soon after my father had died, but if I'd stayed home I wouldn't have made money or seen friends. And I doubted that I'd have recovered faster from grief sitting at home alone.

At one lecture I gave, an attendee who'd heard about my father's death slipped a book into my purse. She said that after her brother's death she'd spent two weeks experiencing something she called "the opposite of a trigger—a *glimmer.*" She said she was suddenly living exclusively in the present. There was no past, no future. She felt like a child. Food tasted incredible. And she said the only thing that really got at what she'd experienced was the book she was giving me, *The Wild Edge of Sorrow:*

Rituals of Renewal and the Sacred Work of Grief. The author, Francis Weller, wrote that being around death gives you "dark wisdom," and he told the Swedish fairy tale of the Lynd Wurm:

A king and queen were having trouble getting pregnant, so they went to a wise old woman for help. The queen didn't follow the directions exactly, and so when she gave birth she had two sons—the first was a worm creature the midwife threw into the woods without anyone knowing. When the prince, who as far as the king and queen knew was their only son, wanted to get married, he found his path blocked by the Lynd Wurm. The monster said the prince could only get married once he was married, as he was the older son. They tried to find him a wife, but he ate all his brides.

Finally, a woman showed up for her wedding night prepared. She carried a bucket of lye and wire brushes and had on seven blouses. She said she would take off a blouse every time he took off a layer of skin. Then she scoured his body with the lye, and he emerged as a human being. They could consummate the marriage and live together happy and whole.

Two moments in this story have haunted me. One is the Lynd Wurm blocking the path. Weller says, "As fairy tales often point out, what was thrown away returns and demands to be acknowledged." The other is what the Lynd Wurm says when his bride tells him to start taking off skins: "No one ever asked me to do that before."

Weller said that is the secret to grief—that we long to have someone ask us to be exposed in that way, to reveal the wildness of our grief, to sit with us in it even if they don't understand it. He described grief as a solitary process that we can't do alone.

My father's death, the divorce, the move, the upending of how I'd envisioned the rest of my life—for as hard as I'd worked to prepare for it—*messed me up*. Grief snuck in around the edges. I'd think, *I'm fine, fine, fine*, and then it would be as though I'd been hit on the head by a falling anvil. Or maybe like I'd put on a lead suit, been tackled, melted like the witch in *The Wizard of Oz*. No analogies worked. Something metal. Something heavy. Bereft.

Hysterical episodes are common when dealing with grief. You're going through your day, and then suddenly lose it on a door that refuses to open or a stranger who won't get out of the way. I thought I was serene until I knocked over a glass while trying to scoot the cat off my keyboard. As water flew everywhere and the cat darted away, I picked up a soggy book and threw it across the room. Then picked it up and threw it *again*. Once I could see straight I looked to see which book it was—*Just Mercy*. Of course it was. I burst out laughing. There I was, alone, knocking things over, flinging objects, laughing and crying at the same time.

The sorrow book told me that I was "doing the work," though I suspected I was just having a nervous breakdown: "Grief pulls us into the underworld, where we are invited to discover a new mode of seeing, one that reveals the holiness of all things." The intensity of grief widens the band of our emotional reality, and so for as much as we can feel sorrow we can now feel joy. Sometimes I cried all day. Some days I was deliriously happy. Other days I went from one extreme to the other in the span of an hour. The greatest joys were having breakfast and dinner with Nate and then the few days a month I went to see David or he came to see me.

"Love does not lead to an end to difficulties," bell hooks wrote, "it provides us with the means to cope with our difficulties in ways that enhance our growth." And yet, growing and changing did not happen in a straight line. I was trying to stay grounded and to take time to grieve and adjust to the changes. I vowed to submit to fate or to the universe or to whatever force I was now beholden to, for which I still had no good words.

And so when I got an email saying that I'd been accepted for a residency at a castle in Scotland, a fellowship that I'd forgotten I applied for, I accepted. I'd never been apart from Nate for more than two weeks, but I figured I'd have to adjust to such separation soon enough, and surely he and Paul could use some time together while I mourned. The deal I made with myself was that when I opened the first notebook in the tall stack from this time of death, divorce, and falling in love, I'd have to read them all in a row; there would be no way out but through.

THIRTY-FIVE

The Castle

Outside the window was a Scottish forest battered by pelting rain and howling wind. Inside, a small bedroom with a dark green carpet and heavy wood and brass furniture, the cold and damp sneaking in around the window frame and under the door. The sun rose straight into my eyes each morning as I sat at my desk, a blanket over my shoulders and my legs as close to the space heater as they could get without burning my skin.

After years of people needing things from me, of duty and service, I suddenly had no responsibility at all, nothing but quiet and time to think. There was no wi-fi and barely any cell service. My lunch—a thermos of soup, a little circle of cheese, a sandwich on brown bread—was delivered to me in a basket outside my door at noon.

Silence was observed from breakfast until dinner, which I ate with my four fellow fellows and the administrator. We chatted and traded books and sipped sherry out of shot glasses or whiskey out of tumblers or red wine out of long-stemmed glasses. We praised the cook and thanked her as we set our napkins on our plates and left the dining room, engaging in a live-action role-play of the nineteenth-century aristocracy.

"Have you ever been alone?" the dramatic Dutch poet asked me as we had a nightcap after dinner in the drawing room. On the wall hung portraits of the former castle inhabitant's friends Jean Cocteau, Truman Capote, and Aldous Huxley.

"I'm alone all day now," I said. "I've never been so alone."

I gestured to my room, where for all but a couple of hours in the evening I sat with my notebooks and occasionally lay down on the green carpet and sobbed. Sinking into the terror of loneliness felt like lowering myself into a hot bath. From a little patch of gravel by the library I'd tried making regular calls the first few days, but after eking out only enough 3G to talk to Nate or

David for a staticky and disappointing few minutes I'd mostly given up.

This was my dream—full days on my own and a private space to work, no meals to make, and no one Duolingo-ing within earshot. So why was I so miserable? Why had I started maniacally talking to myself? Why had I come to think of the residency as writer jail, only instead of gruel there was dry sherry?

I missed Nate. I missed David. I missed Veronica. No one in the castle even touched an arm or hugged; I recalled the phrase "skin hunger." I began having nightmares every night in which I was flying a prop plane over the Atlantic and ran out of fuel.

I started to fear that, now that I was finally free to be with David in a real way, I was going to lose him. He'd given no indication that he wasn't all in. I was the one who'd flown to a foreign country for a month. But I also found myself ruminating on the contrast between how asexual he'd been when we met and how passionate he'd been since. We'd unlocked something in each other; could I really expect to be the sole beneficiary of his erotic awakening? On one of our scratchy calls, I danced around my paranoid imaginings by joking weakly.

"I bet all your female colleagues have your photo pinned up in their lockers," I said.

"You can't be jealous of night-lights when you are the sun," he said.

"Sun or not, I've never been this lonely," I said.

I said I wanted him to come right that minute to Scotland to hold me. I knew it wasn't rational. No visitors were allowed at the castle. It was a busy week for him. He was on a professor's salary, and he couldn't afford to fly internationally at the last minute for a conjugal visit. And yet, that is what I wanted, and that is what I asked for.

He suggested that instead we should wait for our next visit constructively.

"I know!" he said. "Let's do another advent calendar."

They say the things we fall in love with in others are the things that later drive us crazy. I'd fallen in love with David's endless faith in us, his tireless patience, and his reliance on books for wisdom and solace. But as I listened to him through the static of our poor phone connection, I thought of the phrase "philosophy robot." When he started talking about—oh Jesus, not again—*amor fati*, I began to shake. His philosophical approach had returned me to myself. Now it made me want to hurl my phone into a loch.

"In other words, hope and fear are condemned," he said cheerfully, oblivious to my growing horror.

"I'm going to go now," I said with a coldness I'd never felt toward him before.

"Oh," he said, sounding startled. "Do you have to?"

"Yes," I said. "I do."

After hanging up, I walked through the forest around the castle and wondered what had just happened and what it might mean.

I texted Veronica, who said that this reflected my own internal struggles and that I was expecting too much from other people. "You caught a unicorn in David. A kind, smart man who loves you. You don't need a rainbow-colored unicorn, who is also never annoying."

But I was rattled. For the first time, I'd felt something for David other than pure adoration. Once fear crept in, it reduced the stores of love like an object placed in a beaker displaces water. I wasn't sure if my new anger at him meant we'd broken up or that we were doomed. I imagined that when this time at the castle was over I would return home to an apartment full of ghosts, to no husband, no father, and no soulmate either. The recent series of events—that morning in California, the separation from Paul, the death of my father—had been cutting a mooring rope strand by strand. But what was I being liberated from? And what for?

Reentering the castle after my call and long walk, I

kicked off my boots. Sitting at the table in front of me was Martin, one of the other fellows. I hadn't noticed it before, but he looked and talked eerily like my friend Ryan, who I hadn't seen since London. They both had eyes that crinkled when they smiled; both had a dry wit and a tendency to say "darlin'" when they were teasing me.

"You need a hot drink!" Martin said. "You look wind-swept and mournful."

He threw a blanket over my shoulders. "I'll be right back. Don't move."

He returned with tea and a cookie.

"Thank you," I said. I dutifully sipped and ate.

"Hmm," he said, assessing me. "Amazingly, that tea has not completely restored you. I propose we go into town tonight and get obscenely drunk."

"Yes, doctor," I said.

That night he, the other journalist at the castle, and I called a cab. We left the poet fellows behind reading Hungarian novels and hurried down the castle walk, clacking along in our city shoes. Giddy with our sense of freedom, Amy, Martin, and I were acting like kids run-ning away from boarding school rather than respectable professionals just out for dinner.

Amy ordered for us in Chinese while Martin negoti-ated for spicier and more unusual dishes; she let him pick one, spongy latticework tripe with chilis. They talked about their reporting. She was banned from China because of her work. In Africa he'd been thrown in jail and beaten with pistols.

I gazed at them in wonder—my radiant new friends, both with PhDs, crucial reports to file, passports with extra pages. We drank wine with dinner and then we went to a bar, where we had whiskey. Then we went to another bar, where we had beer. When that bar closed, we went to a third bar where we had more beer and perhaps more whiskey and bags of salt-and-pepper potato chips, to which I would have given all the Michelin stars. Martin and I carried on a whole conversation in what I believed at the time to be—but later suspected was not— impeccable French.

In the back seat of the cab back to the castle I was seated in the middle. The three of us merrily chatted away. We recalled how earlier that week, when one of our poet colleagues had said, "I need to practice radical honesty," we all experienced a fight-or-flight reaction. *Do you?* we'd each thought. *Or might radical discretion be more appropriate? Radical flattery? Mitigated honesty?* Riffing on the many options superior to radical honesty, we laughed so hard tears ran down our faces. As we got close to the castle at the end of the half-hour trip I noticed that Martin and I were holding hands.

Once back, we woke up the beleaguered castle administrator, his two-toned beard warped by sleep, and then tromped up the stairs to our floor. Amy went into her room first. Before adjourning to ours, Martin and I stood alone beneath the hall light. I had been in this play before, knew my lines by heart. He looked so much like Ryan had in the London bar light—trustful, happy, expectant. Aside from my hand being held in the cab I hadn't been touched in weeks.

What was David doing back home? Why didn't he miss me enough to fly to Scotland or at least to complain more about us being apart? His infinite patience seemed to be not a virtue but rather a character flaw. And if he truly loved me, surely he'd want me to be held now when he couldn't be there to do it? I was struck by an ugly impulse. If he was going to pelt me with book references while I was suffering, perhaps I should give him something to be philosophical about.

When Nate was two, his pediatrician had explained to me the concept of "object permanence." He'd said that the way toddlers develop it is through constant reality testing. So when they open the kitchen drawer a thousand times a day they're not trying to drive you insane; they want to make sure there are still no monsters in the drawer, only scissors and string.

Given how far apart David and I were and how shut off I felt from his day-to-day and he from mine, I imagined monsters, like the beautiful department colleague who'd said something forward to him at the holiday party. Every time I went to check my email I imagined I'd learn that he'd begun an affair with her. I wanted to go ahead and put a monster in the drawer just to end the suspense. Martin would make a good drawer-monster. Then I'd never have to wonder when one would pop out; I'd know because I'd put it there myself.

And yet, even in my drunkenness and loneliness, I hesitated. The universe had given me sacred sex. I'd made it out of that first hotel room without being incinerated by holy fire. What was I going to do, say, "Thanks for all the mystical visions. I'm also going to continue to fool around with every game and attractive person who crosses my path. Because holy love and thrilling new friendships aren't enough; I also need *intrigue*"? I'd had a mystical experience—why didn't I act like it?

Beyond that: What kind of person did I want to be? Whatever I did, it was between me and myself. I'd have to behave in a way that had integrity, regardless of what anyone else told me I should or shouldn't do. I'd made David no explicit promises. He'd made none to me. But I didn't want to be the kind of person who slept with people when she was in love with someone else, just as I didn't want to be married to someone who wanted me to kiss other men. I wanted how I felt to line up with what I did. If you wanted to be loved, you needed to love. In this situation, what would be the most loving thing to do?

This must have been what David meant when he talked about how the sin does the most damage to the sinner, how cheating was something that corrupted your relationship to yourself more even that it exiled you from your partner. This wasn't about having the moral high ground. It was a question of figuring out who you were and being like that. And I was not, I'd learned, someone who wanted to sleep with anyone but the man I loved, even if he was halfway across the world, almost certainly being groped by nerdishly sexy visiting professors in cardigans and cat-eye glasses.

I hugged Martin, said goodnight, and went back to my little cell, where I switched on my space heater and got under the cold comforter of my twin bed alone, the Whitman paperback on my nightstand.

THIRTY-SIX

The River

A few days after our night out, Martin and I went swimming in the icy forest stream near the castle. I'd never swum in cold water. I suspected it was not for me, but who knew anymore what one liked. And if I was going to try it, why not in a Scottish forest?

As we walked along the narrow path through the woods I explained the concept of sandbags, of trying to stack flirtations around oneself as protection from . . . what exactly? That was what I thought perhaps I would find out in this time of aloneness. I talked about trying not to put monsters in drawers, and how I was trying to feel secure enough not to feel jealous. After talking for a while, willfully mixing metaphors of streetlamps, sandbags, and monsters, I became suddenly horrified that Martin would think I was presuming something.

"I hope you know I'm not saying I thought *you* were interested!" I said. "I'm just rambling."

He smiled cryptically. "Ready?" he said, pointing at the stream.

"Probably not," I said.

We took off our coats and waded into the water. He was wearing a swimsuit. I was wearing pajamas because I hadn't thought to bring a bathing suit to Scotland. The water was so cold it felt like something else, something hard and sharp. As I submerged myself up to my neck I felt all the air rush out of my lungs. I was empty of air and standing in a box of nails. I wondered if this was what death felt like.

I tried to call out to Martin, to ask him why we had done this, but I couldn't speak. I forced my legs to move again and made my way to shore, where I found that I could not feel my body at all. I wrapped myself in towels and sat on the bank of the river, feeling like I'd just drunk eighteen cups of coffee. I started laughing hysterically.

"Right?" he said, smiling and striding calmly out of the water to pick up his own towel.

When I got back to my cell after the first and last cold plunge of my life, I saw a text from him: "For the record, to return to our forest conversation, I certainly *was* interested. But for as drunk as I was the other night and as good as it would have felt to have you in my bed, I went back to my room after that hug and thought, 'I've never done *that* before.' And it seemed to me the perfect end to a lovely night."

If redemption is being presented with an identical situation and making a different choice, that was what I'd done. The kiss with Ryan erased our easy camaraderie. Perhaps by rejecting fleeting pleasures with Martin I'd receive something richer in return. Soon after, almost like a signpost on a hiking trail, Ryan, who I'd been out of touch with for ages, sent me a mixtape with songs about having and not holding or perhaps holding and not having, and it was very good.

In writer jail, I listened to that playlist over and over as I thought of how I'd had things and not had them. I'd been living so much of my life partially. I'd been married but because of lies and sandbags I didn't have what I thought I did. With the mystical experience I'd had the ineffable—the unholdable—for a moment, and then it had gone away. By entertaining the possibility of a pregnancy I'd had the dream of a baby but not the reality. In

loving David from afar, we were together and not together at the same time.

As Martin and I sat in the drawing room with our
peated whiskey, I told him what I was thinking about,
which was how to reconcile what happened with David
and the distance I now felt.

"You are dealing with the aftermath of a Mystical
Sexual Incident!" said Martin. "If this was *Grey's Anatomy*, at the end of the episode Meredith would say, 'You
lose yourself in love and you find yourself in love—'"

"You watch *Grey's Anatomy*?" I said. To my knowledge
he only read massive books in translation.

"The point is: theoretically, yes, love should be infinite
and multiple partners should be possible, but how many
people can you welcome home at night? Love saves and
ruins you. You're all shaken up and unintegrated. That's
a great place to be. Only the boring are certain."

From that moment on, Martin and I were inseparable.
We spent the remaining evenings of our residency cowriting an absurd—and to us, extremely funny—mystery
novel set in the castle. In the drawing room over tea and
at dinner over wine we talked about relationships and
writing and death. We stoked the flames of our new
friendship not with the kindling of stolen glances but
with a long-burning log—our shared belief that at least

one character in our mystery novel should be thrown into a ravine by the administrator for not properly appreciating the genius of Alexander Pope.

Toward the end of the stay, he and I went into Edinburgh for dinner at an "elevated Scottish food" restaurant, one of the best meals of my entire life. Before our dinner, while he got a haircut, I went to a vintage store and found a kilt to bring back for Nate. Then Martin and I went to bookstores and a liquor store to get thank-you gifts for the castle staff. When we returned, we wrapped the gifts while enjoying a nightcap of sherry.

"Do you think we'll ever come back to the castle?" I said as we set the festive packages out on the hall table like it was Christmas eve and we were Santa.

"I'm not sure," he said. "What is the recidivism rate for Scottish castles?"

Sometimes with Martin and sometimes by myself, I walked an hour from the castle to services at the closest church, where the Scottish liturgy demanded that we drive out fear with love. I felt my heart grow lighter. Reading through the stack of notebooks, I came to understand better why things had gone the way they did, and what the point of it all was. As the residency came to an end, I felt ready to reenter the world, no longer a wife or a daughter but rather a woman who believed in love and work and the need to pursue both.

After all the questions I'd asked since I'd started talking to David, I found that only one remained: *What will help me love myself best?* Depending on the moment, the answer might involve action or inaction, expansion or contraction. But it would always be within my power. Only by accepting this responsibility could I become brave enough to do what love demanded.

Rosslyn Chapel, where I sat in a pew praying for love to drive out fear, is where I had this epiphany. It is also where Tom Hanks filmed *The Da Vinci Code.* During the coffee hour after the service, locals dropped his name. They said he was just as nice as everyone says.

THIRTY-SEVEN

Eucatastrophe

Reading W. H. Auden taught me a new word: "eucatastrophe," a neologism Tolkien made out of the Greek for "good" and "sudden turn." It means "a massive turn in fortune from a seemingly unconquerable situation to an unforeseen victory, usually brought by grace rather than heroic effort." That's what began to happen when I returned home.

Letting myself love David, it was as though I'd cast a spell on the world. Holding his hand one day as we sat in his car, I hallucinated that his hand was my hand and mine was his. Joining each other on work trips, we slept intertwined in generic hotel rooms; on visits to each other's homes we began to colonize closets and shelf space.

Sometimes we fell asleep talking and woke up in the middle of the night talking more. Each room became that first one when the lights went off.

David sat with me at my father's memorial service. That night after everyone else had left I made us bowls of ice cream. He and Nate joined forces to mock my love of Magic Shell, the chocolate syrup that hardens when you pour it on ice cream. On his way to bed, Nate hugged him, said goodnight, and David looked at me with shock and delight. How was that for a stroke of fortune no one could have seen coming—he and Nate got along. We loved each other's friends.

There were also misunderstandings and conflicts and tears. In trying to make a spiritual love work day to day, it was as though we'd entered the crystal chamber Superman submits to so he can become human and grow old with Lois Lane. We still couldn't keep our hands off each other, but we were still taking off blouses and scrubbing our skin with lye.

"You're talking to someone else through me," he would say sometimes when I got mad at him. "Probably your father. Because I don't hear myself in what you're describing." There was a lot about living like a monk that he still preferred, and he had a much higher tolerance for skin hunger. I tried not to take it personally, but did not always succeed.

Veronica said, "Here's your mantra: 'I love him. Sometimes his personality stresses me out. It's going to be okay.' And I do think you will be okay. But I also think that it started out so intensely that living in the real world will mean sort of starting over."

"Why can't we just have it be the same as it was but, you know, with us together all the time?" I said.

"Because he's *weird*." She laughed. "You've fallen in love with a wonderful but also very weird person. And now that you're trying to bring your relationship into the real world you've got what musicians call 'demo attachment,' where you get so into the sound of the demo, which is all potential, that you keep comparing it to the fully orchestrated final song."

They say of Shakespeare plays that the way you know if one was a tragedy or a comedy is whether it ended with a death or a wedding. In life, it's harder to tell, because usually a wedding or pregnancy doesn't wrap everything up in a bow of joy. So what does a true happy ending look like? I think it's always a surprise.

"The good that one expects does not come to pass, but unexpected good does," wrote the nineteenth-century French writer Jules Renard. "There is justice, but he who dispenses it is playful. He is a jovial judge, who laughs at us, plays tricks on us, but who, when all is weighed, never makes a mistake."

What proves love is real? What does real even mean? There's no evidence in timelines—whether we stay together for a month or for the rest of our lives. There is no security in living together, nor in having children, nor in wearing rings. All we have at the end of the day is ourselves. Falling in love returned me to myself. I shook my life upside down like an old purse. I put some things into a new purse and left some things out, and that was what I'd carry for some unknown length of time. My only orders now came from Dolly Parton: "Find out who you are and do it on purpose."

Nate brought over friends, who stoically answered questions about where they would be going to college, and we all played Past Lives, a board game from the 1980s that I'd had since high school. You move backward in time, hoping not to lose turns on squares like "100 Years War" while accumulating works of art, historic relics, and "karmic credits," which function like money.

At the end you get a karma points score, a number you look up in *The Book of Past Lives* to learn if you were Joan of Arc or the rat that started the plague, Leonardo da Vinci or Lady Godiva. If you get the maximum number of possible points you learn that you were not a great leader or religious figure. The best score, the highest-level person you can be, is the builder of the pyramids, author of the most profound aphorisms, composer of the most enduring songs: Anonymous.

There's no *happily ever after* when it comes to love—just a swirl, before and after ceremonies of fear and bliss. The point was not that I found a man who could please me. The point was that I learned how to accept pleasure. That, not self-sacrifice, was what it meant to be the more loving one.

I often replay the moment when I knew that everything would be okay. It wasn't in bed with David. It wasn't a scene of domestic tranquility with Nate. It wasn't writing. It was in a moment of transition, making polite conversation with a man who was neither a love interest nor a relative.

The castle administrator was driving me through the Scottish countryside, listening to a classical music show on the BBC and occasionally pointing out sites of interest.

"In that direction is a prep school where the great poet W. H. Auden taught in his youth," he said.

"Really?" I said. "You know, I think about him all the time."

"He was an extraordinary man, and apparently also an excellent teacher."

"Do you know what he cabled back when he was asked to marry Thomas Mann's daughter?"

The administrator turned his head away from the road to look at me, his eyes sparkling. It was as if this proper English gentleman was Life itself, God's own representative on earth. He tossed back his head and said, a look of triumph on his face: "DELIGHTED."

ACKNOWLEDGMENTS

Thank you to:

My grandmother, my mother, and all doers of unhistoric acts.

My former husband for being so gracious about my work and such a conjurer of perfect children. And to those children for being so lovable.

Friends and colleagues who have shared their wisdom with me, whether for an hour or across decades: Alysia Abbott, Syed Ali, Bethany Ball, Carlene Bauer, Aimee Bell, Jen Bergstrom, Jo Brill, Susannah Cahalan, Maureen Callahan, Eric Cleary, Joshua Craze, John Darnielle, Randi Epstein, Isaac Fitzgerald, Tom Hanks, Kathleen Hanna, Logan Hill, Murray Hill, Rae Jacobson, Amy Jordan Jones, Sarah Jones, Abbott Kahler, Louisa Lim, Nola Macek, Tara McKelvey,

Caroline Miller, Ann Morris, Shauna Niequist, Deven Patel, Roland Pearman, Busy Philipps, Katie Raissian, Molly Ringwald, Leah Runyan, Jen Scott, Ivy Shapiro, Lauren Spiegel, Andy Stanton, Meghan Sullivan, Lili Taylor, Nicola Twilley, Don Waring, Jake Wolff, Asia Wong, Jason Zinoman.

Daniel Greenberg of Levine Greenberg Rostan for brilliant agenting, as well as his colleagues Jim Levine, Tim Wojcik, Kerry Sparks, Lindsay Edgecombe, Mike Byrne, and Melissa Rowland for their support.

Rachel A.G. Gilman and Rachel Stone for intrepid assistance.

Everyone at Sob Sisters, Invisible Institute, and *Power Broker* poker night for the fun times.

Dream editor Laura Tisdel for giving my book's soul company—plus everyone at Viking, especially Carlos Zayas-Pons, Jane Cavolina, Andrea Schulz, Molly Fessenden, Jason Ramirez, Kristina Fazzarolo, Magdalena Deniz, Sharon Gonzalez, and Brian Tart.

Booksellers everywhere, including Mitchell Kaplan, Hannah Oliver Depp, Kelly Justice, Kira Wizner, Josh Christie, Danny Caine, Scott Abel, Jake Cumsky-Whitlock, Ben Nockels, Jeff Martin, and Saint Emma Straub.

Festival- and fair-throwers, with extra love to Lissette Mendez.

Every last librarian, particularly Melanie Locay and Rebecca Federman at the New York Public Library Research Study Rooms; Carolyn Waters at the Society Library; everyone at the British Library; and the staff of the NYPL's Tompkins Square, Jefferson Market, and Ottendorfer branches, with extra gratitude to Jeffrey Katz, Corinne Neary, and Kristin Kuehl.

The Only Ones' Peter Perrett for writing such a good song and warmly granting permission to quote from it.

Hawthornden Castle and its elegant administrator, Hamish Robinson.

A teacher who changed my life; from Clarice Lispector: "Everything comes to an end but what I'm writing to you goes on. Which is good, very good. The best is not yet written. The best is between the lines."